"Lucien, I shake of her head.

"You can't...can't what?"

"Marry you."

"What?"

"Don't you see? This isn't going to work. You're the one that hasn't figured it out yet."

Lucien pulled on the lines, bringing the horse to a stop. "See here, Billie, you can't assume something like that. You have no idea how I feel about you." He blinked a few times. "Well, you should have a good inkling by now. If you don't, then you need to take a second look."

"And you need to look at this!" Throwing caution to the wind in her frustration, she pulled off her eyepatch.

He stared, just like anyone would. But he didn't flinch, or make a face. He didn't even gasp in shock.

Billie sat and waited, then waited some more. "Well?"

Kit Morgan has written all her life. Her whimsical stories are fun, inspirational, sweet and clean, and depict a strong sense of family and community. Raised by a homicide detective, one would think she'd write suspense, but no. Kit likes fun and romantic Westerns! Kit resides in the beautiful Pacific Northwest in a little log cabin on Clear Creek, after which her fictional town that appears in many of her books is named.

The
GROOM'S
UNLIKELY MATCH

KIT MORGAN

Previously published as *Dear Mr. Miller*

Recycling programs
for this product may
not exist in your area.

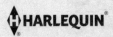

ISBN-13: 978-1-335-62998-2

The Groom's Unlikely Match

First published in 2018 as Dear Mr. Miller by Kit Morgan.
This edition published in 2020.

This edition published by arrangement with Harlequin Books S.A.

For questions and comments about the quality of this book,
please contact us at CustomerService@Harlequin.com.

Harlequin Enterprises ULC
22 Adelaide St. West, 40th Floor
Toronto, Ontario M5H 4E3, Canada
www.Harlequin.com

Printed in U.S.A.

The
GROOM'S
UNLIKELY MATCH

Chapter One

La Maison Pettigrew, Denver, Colorado, 1901

Fantine Leblanc finished her breakfast, left the kitchen and began her day.

She stopped in the hall and studied her reflection in a small mirror on the wall. Her employer, *Madame* Adelia Pettigrew, had regaled her with another fantastic tale yesterday, about a man named Oscar White who married a mail-order bride called (not a joke) Lily Fair. She'd been horribly burn-scarred, her body disfigured, but her face was untouched and still beautiful. And Oscar had loved her despite (or maybe because of) her flaws.

The story made Fantine think about the previous stories her employer shared with her—about Daniel Weaver, Eli Turner, Major Comfort (also not a joke) and Fletcher Vander, all of whom had received a beautiful bride via *Madame* Pettigrew's mail-order service. Okay, Mr. Comfort received a bride he didn't send for, which led to all sorts of twists and turns, but nonetheless each man married a pretty woman and were now quite happy.

But had Mrs. Pettigrew ever sent off a *homely* bride? Perhaps she should ask.

She went into her employer's office and studied the walls, covered with framed letters from happy wives. If *Madame* Pettigrew had sent off a less-than-pretty bride, how did her story turn out? Was the groom disappointed? Did things work between them? Did they fall in love?

Another mirror graced one wall here. Fantine crossed the room and stared at her reflection. She didn't consider herself beautiful, but she wasn't hideous either. And what were looks if the heart was pure? Could a handsome man fall in love with an ugly woman? Well... perhaps "ugly" was too strong a word. What about "unattractive"? No, that meant the same thing...

"What are you doing, *ma petite*?"

Fantine gasped and spun to face her. "*Madame* Pettigrew, I did not hear you come in."

Her employer eyed her a moment. "Obviously not. What were you doing? Why were you looking at yourself with such..." She made a circular motion with her hand. "...scrutiny?"

Fantine looked at the floor. "Because... I do not think I am beautiful."

"*Pardon?* What do you mean? Of course you are beautiful!"

"No, *Madame*, I am not. Though I do not think I am ugly."

"Well, that is a relief," Mrs. Pettigrew said as she went to her desk and sat. She picked up a stack of letters and shoved them toward Fantine. "See that these get posted today."

"Yes, *Madame.*" Fantine sat in the chair on the other side of the desk. "Do you wish to dictate any letters this morning?"

"No, I have applications to sort through." She reached for another stack of letters with a weary sigh.

"Anything wrong, *Madame* Pettigrew?"

Her employer studied her. "Why do you think you are not beautiful?"

Fantine's mouth dropped open. It was one thing for her to think of herself as undesirable, another for someone else to voice it. "Um…well, I am too thin…"

"Eat different foods" was Mrs. Pettigrew's calm reply.

"My eyes are too big…"

"Your eyes are easily read and full of the innocence of youth. I think they are your best feature."

"They are?"

"Of course? Anything else of yours you'd like to disparage?"

Fantine looked away. "No, *Madame.*"

Mrs. Pettigrew sighed again. "What brought this on, *ma belle*?"

Fantine, eyes still averted, clasped her hands in her lap. "The last tale you told, the one about Oscar White?"

"What about it?"

Fantine looked at her. "Lily Fair was so scarred, yet still beautiful in face and form. Would Oscar have loved her if *all* of her had been scarred?"

Mrs. Pettigrew sat back in her chair and folded her hands in front of her. "So that is what bothers you," she stated.

"But I have not said anything…"

"You did not have to, *ma rose*." She drummed her fingers against the back of her hand before continuing. "You wish to marry one day, *oui*?"

Fantine wasn't sure what to say. What if she said yes and lost her position? But she couldn't lie. "I do."

"Of course you do. You are young, with many years ahead of you. Why would you not want to marry?" She glanced at the walls around them, then pointed. "Fetch me that gold-framed letter over there."

Fantine rose, got the letter and brought it back to the desk. "What bride is this?"

Mrs. Pettigrew smiled.

"*Madame?*" Fantine urged, retaking her seat.

"The tale behind this letter will make you think of yourself differently, *ma petite*."

"How so, *Madame?*"

She smiled again. "You will see…"

Nowhere, Washington Territory, March 1877

Dear Mrs. Pettigrew,
I write to you in answer to an advertisement I came across regarding mail-order brides. I am acquainted with several men in the area whom are happily married to such women, and as the local population of single females is severely limited at present, I find it advantageous to utilize your service.
About myself: I am twenty-six years of age and a hair over six feet tall, with black hair and grey eyes. I hail from a small town in the Washington Territory by the name of Nowhere. The mainstay

of the farmers here is apples, along with a few other fruit crops. It is beautiful country, very different from New Haven, Connecticut, where I am originally from. I am a banker, educated at Yale, and would do well with a woman in possession of an intellect similar to my own.

That said, I am not sure what caliber of women utilize your service. I've met only one: Ebba Weaver, the wife of Daniel Weaver, a local orchard owner. Ebba tells me she has written to you and told you of her wedding and subsequent events. It has been almost a year since Daniel and Ebba wed, and they could not be happier. Nellie Davis, the woman that caused Ebba so much trouble, is still performing community service as penance for her crime.

But I digress. I seek an educated woman with whom I can hold intelligent conversations, one skilled in the domestic arts, with a strong demeanor and constitution. As an aside, I am partial to taller women. I would appreciate your expertise and discretion when sorting through candidates in search of my potential future bride.
Yours truly,
Lucien Miller

Lucien folded his letter carefully, put it into a pre-addressed envelope and sealed it. "Now to post."

He rose from his chair, straightened a book and a few other objects on his desk before grabbing his coat and hat. His home was new and small, a little cottage on the edge of town, and he was still putting the finishing touches on it. It was modest considering his position as the new vice-president of the local bank…but then the bank itself, like the town of Nowhere, was modest. He found it satisfactory.

Besides, he didn't want to invest in a larger home as he wasn't sure how long he would stay in Nowhere. He wanted a wife, and if he couldn't get one here he'd go elsewhere—Seattle, perhaps, or Portland. Even Baker City had more women than Nowhere.

But a conversation with Arlan Weaver at Quinn's Mercantile last month got him thinking. Arlan and his three younger brothers had sent away for mail-order brides. So had Clayton and Spencer Riley and Warren Johnson, and to his knowledge each man was happily married. Many of them had children now. Calvin Weaver acquired an entire family when his wife's seven younger siblings came to live with them—quite the brood, but nothing the Weavers couldn't handle.

Ever since the wedding of Daniel, the youngest Weaver brother, last year, Lucien had felt a gnawing in his gut that wouldn't go away. He wouldn't call it loneliness so much as an annoying emptiness—and it was growing worse. But then, he'd never felt lonely, not even as an only child. He'd always had friends, knew how to keep busy, and was his own best company. As he'd never get rid of himself, this was good news.

Now, however, he wanted more. He wanted to share his life with another, and the only natural course he could think of (other than getting a dog) was to wed. Besides, he wanted to converse with a companion, not just feed one. And he was getting awful tired of his own cooking and that of Hank's restaurant. The help there wasn't always as accommodating as it ought to be either—thank Heaven Nellie Davis's community service would be over in a few months.

Hank wasn't happy about losing the free help, but Nellie was eager to be done—and frankly, so were a lot of Hank's customers. Nellie had been sentenced to a year of serving in Hank's restaurant after arguing with Judge Whipple during a trial involving Ebba and Daniel Weaver and Stanley Oliver. Mr. Oliver was convicted of attempted rape and sentenced to two years on McNeil Island, a nasty place but no less than he deserved. And Hank's patrons had been sentenced to a year of Nellie's inept and grudging "service."

Lucien left home and walked to Quinn's Mercantile to post his letter. Nowhere was small, and slow to keep up with the world's progress. It had a telegraph office now, but still lacked a post office.

Sheriff Spencer Riley appreciated the telegraph, though, especially since an outlaw gang had been harassing stagecoaches and trains between Seattle and Boise over the last year. Being right in the middle, the people of Nowhere were on edge. Spencer had tried to keep the news under wraps, but Nellie had overheard Spencer and Clayton while serving them breakfast and now the whole town knew. Ironically, Nellie had earned her one-year sentence for gossiping. She seemed far from rehabilitated.

"Good morning, Lucien," Matthew Quinn called from behind the counter as he entered.

Lucien strolled over and set his letter down. "Good morning, Matthew. I need a stamp."

"Right away. Your letter will go out in Monday's…" He stopped short as he read the address. "Mrs. Petti-grew? Isn't that…"

"Yes, the same woman who sent your cousin Daniel his bride."

"Well, I'll be." Matthew picked up the letter. "You're sending for a mail-order bride?"

"Yes, but I'd appreciate it if you kept this to yourself for now. Who knows how long this will take? Mrs. Pettigrew might not find anyone suitable for a while, and I don't want to be bombarded with questions from all and sundry in the meantime. Particularly not your mother-in-law—no offense."

"None taken—I understand," Matthew said with a nod. "I won't even tell Charlotte."

"You won't tell me what?" Charlotte Quinn asked as she joined him behind the counter. Before either man could speak, she spotted the envelope. "Lucien Miller, are you sending off for a mail-order bride?"

Lucien rolled his eyes and softly groaned. "It's not to be common knowledge, Mrs. Quinn. I beg of you."

"Oh, stop with the 'Mrs. Quinn'—Charlotte will do. You've been in town long enough."

"My apologies," he said. "I know how people can get you and your mother-in-law mixed up."

"True," she agreed. "Well, I'm happy for you. Mrs. Pettigrew sent Daniel a wonderful bride."

"Yes, Ebba and Daniel are very happy. How is she doing, by the way? Is it true she's in the family way?"

"Yes, isn't it wonderful?" Charlotte said, then froze. "Lucien, where did you hear it from? We haven't told anyone outside the family."

"Your mother informed me as she served my lunch yesterday."

Matthew tapped the envelope. "Which is why he was swearing me to secrecy about this."

Charlotte closed her eyes and shook her head. "She'll never learn." She picked up a feather duster. "But I won't say a word, Lucien. You can count on me."

"Thank you, I appreciate it." He glanced around at the various goods.

"Do you need anything?" Matthew asked.

"I was thinking about dishes. I have but a few. If I'm to have a wife, she'll want more, don't you think?"

"Oh yes." Charlotte came around the counter. "Let me show you what we have. You could also order a nice set—you have time."

"Yes, I'm sure I do. How long did it take for the last few brides to show up?"

"Hmm, let's see…those would be the Weaver brides. Benjamin's showed up after the preliminary letters were exchanged. Calvin's took longer, which meant an extra letter here and there. To be honest, it's getting harder to keep track. And we all know what happened with Daniel and Ebba…"

Lucien and Matthew nodded without comment, and Lucien cringed. Mrs. Pettigrew had unwisely added a single sentence to Ebba's first and only letter to Daniel. That one line, read by none other than Nellie Davis, caused a heap of trouble that Nellie was still paying for—apparently to no avail.

"I can show you the catalogue we order from," Matthew offered, shaking Lucien from his thoughts.

"Yes, please do." The few pieces of china the mercantile had were rather dull, just blue and white. "I've seen red-and-white patterns back east. Do they have those in the catalogue?"

"Yes, as I recall," Charlotte said. "Pink and white, too."

"Pink, you say? Women like pink, don't they?"

"Some do. Myself, I'm partial to blue. And violet."

"You are?" he said, intrigued.

Charlotte smiled in amusement. "What else are you unsure of when it comes to a woman's likes?"

Lucien shrugged. "If I'm to be honest, most everything."

She nodded. "That's what I thought. Come along and let's look at that catalogue."

Meanwhile, on a lonely road in New Jersey...

"Father!"

Captain Andrew Sneed clutched his daughter's hand. "Jane, you're bleeding!" he rasped.

"So are you." She put her hand over the wound in his belly. "Hang on, I have to fix this."

"Your...your face, child," he said, weaker now.

"Hush, I have to staunch the flow." She reached into her sleeve and pulled out a handkerchief—it was all she had. She cursed under her breath and lifted her skirt.

"Jane," her father whispered. "You can do nothing for me now."

"Don't say that!" She ripped at her petticoats to make a bandage.

"My darling daughter, I am..." He took a deep breath. "...dying. You must let me go."

"No! I'll save you!" She wadded the strip of cloth and pressed it over his wound.

"You must...take care of yourself. Your eye..."

"Never mind about it. I... I...your life is more important." She saw his blood spread through the piece of petticoat and pressed harder. She felt lightheaded, and wondered how much blood she'd lost. The bilge rat that shot her father had also slashed her face with a huge knife. He didn't want to kill her—if he had, he'd have shot her too. He must've had other plans for her, and she could just guess what.

She glanced at the unconscious heap lying nearby. The highwayman's comrades had killed the driver of their coach, robbed them and left him to do his worst to her. She counted herself lucky—they could have stayed behind, each taking a turn once her assailant slaked his own lust. Instead he'd decided to be alone with her—and she hoped she'd made him pay for that.

"Jane," her father rasped. "My little Billie…"

She looked into his eyes in the bright moonlight. "Father, hold on…"

"I can't. No sense now." He swallowed hard. "Promise me…"

"What, Father?" she asked and gripped his hand.

"Promise me you'll marry, have children, a good life."

Marry! The word sent a chill up her spine. No man had ever shown an interest in marrying her. Besides, she might not live long enough to…

"Promise me!"

She gripped his hand harder and pressed her ripped petticoat against the wound in his belly. "I promise." Tears spilled over her left cheek; her right was covered in blood. She'd have to do something about that and quickly, but first she had to save her father. "Please hold on!"

He managed a smile. "You are the most precious treasure…in my possession. We still have a little money…"

"Shhh, please don't talk," she said, her voice cracking.

"Use it to find a husband. Go west, like we planned…"

She buried her face in his chest to stifle a sob. It didn't work.

"Promise me, Billie."

Her head came up, making her dizzy. She couldn't see out of her right eye and wondered if she ever would again. "Yes, yes, I promise. I'll marry, I'll go west, I'll…"

Her father's head lolled to the side.

"Father?" She put her ear to his chest. Silence. "Father?!"

Billie Jane Sneed grabbed her father by the coat and shook him, but to no avail. He was gone.

Chapter Two

Denver, Colorado, April 1877

> *I am a banker, educated at Yale, and would do well with a woman in possession of an intellect similar to my own…*

Mrs. Pettigrew referred to the letter in her hand, then studied the woman standing before her. "Hm, perhaps," she mused.

"Perhaps what?" the woman snapped in a British accent.

Mrs. Pettigrew's eyes narrowed. "Why do you resist, *ma belle*?" she asked. "How do you expect me to find you a husband, when you keep rejecting all of my applicants?"

"Because this is hopeless!" Billie said. "Look at me!"

Mrs. Pettigrew looked the girl over. "I see nothing wrong."

"Nothing? I'm the size of an oak tree, blind in one

eye, scarred and half the men in Denver think I'm a pirate!"

"Perhaps if you would refrain from dressing as a sailor, you would not attract such comparisons?"

Billie glanced at her clothing—she'd put on her father's old captain's uniform for this appointment because, frankly, it was the nicest outfit she had. There wasn't a dress in the world that she looked good in, and since she'd been working odd jobs as she made her way west, wearing men's clothing was just more practical. But certainly Mrs. Pettigrew had a point.

After she and her father were set upon by highwaymen—stage robbers, they were referred to in this country—she'd been doing her best to make her money last. She'd lost far more than money during that robbery—she'd lost her father, the only family she had. She'd promised him she would marry, have a good life and children, and was now trying to pursue that.

Problem was, she was no beauty, at least in her eyes. Her minimal number of suitors back home in London had agreed. Of course, if her father had been rich, she'd have been married long ago, beauty or no beauty. Probably also miserable, for what man would marry her for love, or any other reason other than money? At least she still had the fortitude to carry out his dying wish, but how many men were looking for fortitude?

"But come now, you must not be so hard on yourself," Mrs. Pettigrew went on. "You are…statuesque! *Oui?*"

Billie rolled her remaining eye. If the comrades of the murdering wretch that killed him hadn't come back, he'd have paid dearly for his crimes. As it was, she'd only been able to knock him unconscious with a rock—

just as he slashed her face with a knife. He fell and so did she, her face stinging like the devil. She'd thought the wound would hurt more, then remembered something her father told her: *It's the fatal wounds that fool a man, Billie Jane. Those are the ones to beware of, the ones with no pain...*

The wound to her face began to hurt a lot. Or maybe it had all along, but she'd been so busy trying to keep her father from bleeding to death, she'd paid little attention to her own pains. Then she'd had to take refuge under a fallen log when his murderer's compatriots returned to see what was taking him so long. They'd ridden away with the unconscious form of her father's killer, leaving her with his dead body—and wounds far deeper than a knife could make.

Billie reached up and touched the rough eyepatch she wore. The scar on her forehead and right cheek wasn't so bad, but doctors couldn't save her eye. They'd half-blinded her, and made her bitter. She hoped that at least her and her father's attacker had died from the blow she'd dealt him. Would serve him right...

"*Ma petite*," Mrs. Pettigrew began.

"Don't call me that! There's nothing *little* about me."

The matchmaker sighed and studied her. "*Est-ce que parle français?*"

Billie frowned and took a deep breath through the nose. Mrs. Pettigrew's French wasn't exactly perfect. "*Oui, je le parle couramment.*"

"Why, that is wonderful!" Mrs. Pettigrew declared. "You are fluent in the French!" She looked at the letter in her hand. "This gentleman wishes an educated woman. Do you speak any other languages?"

"*Ich spreche Deutsch*," Billie said on a sigh.

"Two languages! Superb! Where did you go to school, my dear?"

Billie's smile was sardonic. "On the deck of my father's ship, mostly."

Mrs. Pettigrew's eyes grew wide. "What is this? You sailed with your father?"

"Not all the time—it depended on the crew. But yes, often enough."

Mrs. Pettigrew gave her an appreciative smile. "I think you will suit *Monsieur* Miller nicely. But those clothes…" She began to walk a circle around Billie. "These will never do."

"I keep these clothes because…" Billie stopped herself. There were several reasons, aside from being unable to find a dress that didn't look like she was wearing a Bedouin's tent. It was a way to remember her father. They were more convenient for working. And perhaps because after her ordeal, she was afraid of men, and it was safer to dress and act like one.

No, not perhaps. With her hair stuffed under a cap and her eyepatch and scars, she easily passed for a bloke. Not to mention her height and build—she was just over six feet and wide-boned to boot. Of course, she was also large in other places that marked her a woman—buxom, with a fundament big enough to keep things in balance. Those aspects, she had to hide as best she could while, say, digging ditches all day.

Mrs. Pettigrew pulled at her peacoat. "Take this off, *ma belle*. Let me see you."

Billie shrugged off her coat, then, at the other woman's prompting, her shirt. Underneath, she was wrapped up tight as an Egyptian mummy.

But Mrs. Pettigrew could see past the winding cloths.

"*Mon Dieu*, you are, er…well-endowed." Mrs. Petti-grew walked another circle around her. "In more places than one."

She rolled her eyes. "Some of my father's friends used to call me Buxom Billie."

"That is not a bad thing. Many men desire such a woman. Especially one who is tall and strong."

Billie turned to her in disbelief. "Really?" she scoffed. "I've yet to meet one."

"Clearly you are new to the West." Mrs. Pettigrew went to her desk and pulled a reticule out of a drawer. "Come, get dressed. We are leaving."

"What? Where are we going?"

Mrs. Pettigrew went to a bell-pull and gave it a tug. "Shopping. You cannot meet *Monsieur* Miller dressed like an able seaman. We must make you into something special, worthy of your womanly charms!"

Billie glanced at her chest while re-buttoning her shirt. "Surely you jest."

Mrs. Pettigrew's eyes narrowed again as she smiled. "I do not jest, *ma belle*. Now let us go! We will pay a visit to my personal *modiste*!"

Billie's eyes widened. "But Mrs. Pettigrew, I haven't the money for such things."

Adelia Pettigrew sniffed and smiled. "But I do."

Vincenza de la Rosa (Vini for short, and short she was) peered at Billie through a *lorgnette*. If Billie were compacted to five feet tall, she might look like the short, squat woman, but she still moved gracefully. Billie mar-veled at the speed with which she hopped onto a stool to study her new charge. "This is a tall one!" she ex-claimed. "And…wide."

Billie fumed. "Excuse me?"

"She meant nothing by it, *ma cherie*," Mrs. Pettigrew soothed. She turned to Mrs. de la Rosa. "What do you think, Vini?"

"I think this will be expensive. So much fabric…"

Billie made a fist and wondered how long she'd spend in gaol for punching the woman in the face.

"She is tall but proportionate, no?"

Mrs. de la Rosa nodded. "She could get away with not wearing a bustle."

"Did you hear that?" Mrs. Pettigrew gushed. "No bustle!"

Billie's expression was flat. "I heard."

Mrs. Pettigrew continued to smile as the *modiste* pulled a notebook and pencil out of nowhere and started to jot things down. "We'll need shoes," she told Vini. "And other accessories."

Billie's expression changed to panic. "But Mrs. Pettigrew, I…"

"Yes, yes, I know. You have no money."

Mrs. de la Rosa snapped to attention. "No money?!"

Billie willed herself not to cringe. She hated charity, and had decided on the carriage ride to the shop that she'd find a way to pay the matchmaker back, every bloody cent.

"Pish-tosh—I am taking care of this," Mrs. Pettigrew stated sternly.

Mrs. de la Rosa calmed. "Well, that is another matter. We continue." She hopped off the stool, went to the counter, picked up a small bell and rang it.

A pretty young blonde with big blue eyes rushed in and curtsied. "Yes, Mrs. de la Rosa?"

"Measure this woman, Maitred. I will be in my office discussing details with *Signora* Pettigrew."

"Yes, ma'am." The girl pulled a measuring cloth out of her apron pocket. She was no taller than her employer and studied Billie as if she didn't know where to start.

"Use the stool," Billie suggested dourly. "You might as well start at the top and work your way down."

Maitred smiled weakly. "Yes, ma'am." She stepped onto the stool and got to work-measuring Billie's full height, her neck, the breadth of her shoulders. Billie felt more like she was being fitted for a suit than a dress—which would've suited her just fine.

"Oh dear," Maitred said when she went to measure her bust and found nothing but wrapping. "This could pose a problem."

"Just a moment," Billie grumbled. At least they had her in the back room for modesty's sake. It took a couple of minutes to unwrap her chest, and once she did poor Maitred gasped at the size of it. Billie sighed, partly at the girl's reaction and partly because it was a relief to have the dratted bindings off. Maybe she'd still look like she was wearing a tent in the end, but a camisole would have to feel better than what she was used to.

Maitred kept on measuring, occasionally jotting a measurement in her notebook. When she got to Billie's hips, she checked for padding, then yelped in delight as she finished measuring. "You are perfectly proportionate, ma'am. Your bust and hips are the same."

"How nice," she said, unable to keep the sarcasm out of her voice. She knew how she was built. She also knew Mrs. Pettigrew hadn't lied—there were men out there that liked a woman of her proportions, and some of them even liked her height. What they didn't like was that she had a mind and could think for herself. She was no damsel in distress, and woe betide the fellow who tried to treat her as one. She pushed the thought aside, lest she back out of this mail-order madness and go work as a stagecoach driver.

"You are so wonderfully tall," Maitred said. "If you don't mind my saying."

Billie stared at her. "You think it's wonderful."

"Yes, I wish I was taller. I hate being so small."

"If it's any consolation, I hate being so large."

"Maybe we could meet in the middle," Maitred suggested. "Then we'd both have what we want."

Billie smiled. "If only we could. But at least you can put on heeled shoes. What can I do, stoop like a hunchback?"

Maitred nodded sadly. "We make the best of what the good Lord gave us."

"Yes. We've little choice." She watched the assistant scribble in her notebook and return it to her apron. "Where are you from, Maitred? You have an unusual name."

"Massachusetts, originally. Nantucket."

"Really? I've heard of it. Was your father a sailor?"

Maitred nodded. "On a whaler. You're from England?"

"Cornwall, to be precise," Billie said. "But I spent a lot of time in London. And my father was a sea captain."

Maitred clapped in delight. "It's such a pleasure to meet you! I'm Maitred Hubble. As to my name, my father gave it to me, but I don't know where he got it from. He died soon after I was born—lost at sea—and never told my mother its origins."

"I'm sorry," Billie said as her eyes drifted away. "I lost my father too. Not long ago."

"Oh, I'm sorry to hear, miss…"

"Call me Billie. Billie Jane Sneed, at your service."

"Billie, then. Your mother?"

"Died giving birth to me." She swallowed hard. She might as well be wearing a sign that said *I KILLED MY MUM.* She didn't grow up to be large, she was born that way. Her father was big too, but her mother wasn't. From her father's description, she was no bigger than Maitred.

Maitred now stood, staring at her eyepatch with big blue eyes. "My mother's gone too," Maitred said quickly. "Consumption, last year."

"I'm so sorry. How old are you?"

"Eighteen, come September."

Billie glanced around the well-appointed dressing room. "And you want to be a dressmaker?"

"Oh, more than anything."

Billie envied her. Maitred had a job she loved, was set up in a well-to-do shop and on her way to fulfilling her dream. Where was she? Getting gussied up to be mailed to some man in a town literally called Nowhere.

"I'd like to get married one day," Maitred added tentatively. "Mrs. de la Rosa doesn't want me to—she'd rather I work long hours for her."

Billie's eyes flicked to the door and back. "I see." She bent to get eye-to-eye with the girl. "If you want to be a dressmaker, then be a dressmaker with your own shop. If you want to get married, then you get married."

Maitred smiled as Billie straightened. "I always thought it was one or the other."

"Not hardly. You just need to know what you want, then make it happen." She went to a chair and sat. "You're lucky. At least you know."

"And you don't?"

Billie looked at her. "No. I know what my father wanted."

Before Maitred could reply, Mrs. Pettigrew and Mrs. de la Rosa returned to the dressing room. "Wonderful news, *ma belle*," Mrs. Pettigrew said. "We will have several outfits made—they will be ready next week."

Billie flushed red. "You didn't have to commission so many…"

"Nonsense! You must be well prepared to meet *Monsieur* Miller. He is a banker, after all."

Well, Billie thought as she began re-wrapping herself, that's something. But those kinds of men didn't usually want a woman like her—they wanted a pretty doll like Maitred to show off to their friends at social gatherings. She would never do in that capacity. "Mrs. Pettigrew…what happens if Mr. Miller doesn't like me?"

Mrs. Pettigrew and Maitred stared at her in shock. Mrs. de la Rosa nodded in agreement. "How can you say such a thing?" Mrs. Pettigrew asked. "Look at you! You are beautiful!"

Billie closed her eyes. She wished the woman would stop saying that! "Mrs. Pettigrew, I know what I look like. And I know there's not much anyone can do about it."

"But that is where you are wrong." She wagged a finger at her. "You have given Vini much to work with! You will be her greatest triumph!" She turned to the *modiste*. "Is that not true, Vini?"

Mrs. de la Rosa froze for a moment, swallowed. "Why, er…yes." She looked Billie up and down. "My greatest triumph." She put a hand to her chin and stroked it a few times. "Maitred! The purple velvet, quick!" Maitred ran from the room as Mrs. de la Rosa began to circle Billie. "I will make you a traveling suit fit for a queen!"

"I'd settle for one fit for the train to where this Mr. Miller lives." She looked at Mrs. Pettigrew. "Is it really called *Nowhere*?"

Her new-found benefactor laughed and tossed her hands in the air. "*Certainement!*"

Billie sighed. "Figures." She thought a moment as the two women circled and conversed about different fabrics. "At least in a place called Nowhere, I can count on even a banker being a man of modest ambition."

Mrs. Pettigrew laughed. "Do not assume."

"Why not? I'm sure he's making all sorts of assumptions as to what kind of bride he has coming."

"Perhaps, but we will surprise him, *oui*?"

For the first time in a long time, Billie laughed. "Oh, he'll be surprised all right." She just hoped the poor bloke didn't die of shock when he saw her.

Chapter Three

Nowhere, Washington Territory, May 1877

"Lucien, what are you doing out here?" Spencer Riley asked as he stepped out of the sheriff's office. "Did you need somethin'?"

Lucien had been standing by Spencer's open door. "No, I'm waiting for the stage."

"My mistake," Spencer said. "I'm not used to seeing you around town this time of day. You're usually at work. Relative paying you a visit? Great time of year for it." Indeed it was. Once May came around, the weather grew warmer, the air sweetened with the scent of budding fruit orchards. No wonder Spencer had his door open.

"Er, no," Lucien said. He hadn't told anyone else he had a mail-order bride coming, and true to her word, Charlotte hadn't either. Once she arrived, he'd have to tell the town preacher and his wife, and then everyone would know. But he wanted a few days to get to know his bride first. No sense rushing into these things.

"Bank business, then? Do I need to be aware of anything?"

"No, this isn't bank business. It's…personal. Private."

"I was just wondering." Spencer looked down the street as Lucien was doing, craning his neck. "You nervous?"

Lucien jumped. "Me? Nervous? Why?"

Spencer shrugged. "Just asking."

"Hey, Sheriff Riley!" someone called from across the street.

Spencer smiled and cringed at the same time. "Howdy, Calvin. What are you doing in town?"

Calvin Weaver strolled toward them with the most beautiful woman within a hundred miles on his arm. His wife Isabella was Italian, and the most gorgeous creature any man in Nowhere had ever seen. Lucien tipped his hat. "Mrs. Weaver, Calvin."

"Howdy, Luce!" Calvin slapped him hard on the back.

Lucien coughed in response. If he'd hit him any harder, he'd have knocked the wind out of him. "Hello," he replied stiffly.

"Is the bank not open today?" Mrs. Weaver asked in her Italian accent.

Lucien found it enchanting. He liked conversing with the woman and her siblings—all seven of them—when they came to town. "It is. Mr. Davis and the other employees are there."

"*He's* waiting for the stage," Spencer volunteered, peering down the street again.

Calvin and Isabella did the same. "Relations comin' for a visit?" Calvin asked. "That's nice."

"Not a relative," Spencer tossed in.

Lucien furrowed his brow. "Nor is it banking business," he said before the sheriff could.

Calvin and Isabella glanced at each other, then looked at Lucien. "Then who is it?" they asked at once.

Lucien sighed, just as Calvin's older brother Arlan and Isabella's younger sister Rufina jumped onto the boardwalk. "Howdy, everybody!" Arlan said and, as was the Weaver way, slapped Lucien on the back. He smacked Spencer just as hard, pitching him forward an inch or two in the process. At least Lucien stayed on his feet. Arlan was huge! "What's everyone doin' standin' 'round?" the eldest Weaver asked.

"Waiting for the stage," Lucien quickly said. "And no, it's not a relative or any bank business."

Everyone looked at him. "Then what is it for?" Rufi asked. She was pretty like her older sibling, her Italian accent almost as thick.

Lucien pulled out his pocket watch, looked at it, then stuffed it back in his vest pocket. "Personal business."

"Ya look nervous," Arlan told him.

"Not at all," Lucien said, willing himself to stay calm. He might as well get this over with. "Fine—if you must know, I'm waiting for my mail-order bride."

"Mail-order bride?!" the men cried, exchanging astonished looks.

Isabella and Rufi smiled. "A bride—how wonderful!" Isabella said.

"What's wonderful is that my mother isn't around," Spencer added. "You all know how she gets when there's a new bride in town."

Calvin and Arlan laughed. "Yer ma and our aunt Betsy," Arlan said.

"Yeah, won't they be surprised when they find out they missed one!" Calvin added.

"Thank Heaven for that," Spencer muttered under his breath. There hadn't been a wedding in town since Arlan and Calvin's younger brother Daniel's the previous summer. Leona Riley and Betsy Quinn loved a wedding—and pity the poor bride that fell into their well-meaning clutches. That way lay madness.

"Then you'll understand if I ask you not to mention this to your mother too soon?" Lucien said to Spencer.

"You have my word," he said with a smile.

Lucien breathed easier. "Thank you."

"Congratulations," Isabella said. "We picked a good time to come to town."

Rufi gave Lucien a shy smile. "Yes, congratulations."

Calvin reached over and gave a strand of her long hair a tug. "One day ya'll get married too. But ya ain't gonna be no mail-order bride."

"Says who?" she asked defiantly. Despite being a recent arrival, Rufi had picked up the Western American dialect quickly.

Her sister laughed. "For one, *sorella*, we are already out in the West."

"And 'cause none of us could stand it if ya left." Arlan pulled her into a bear hug and tickled her.

Rufi laughed and squirmed out of his embrace. "I am not ready to marry anyway."

"True—ya ain't old enough," Calvin replied.

"I am so! I am seventeen next month!"

"Don't matter. Yer not gettin' hitched 'til yer sister and I say so."

"Stop it," Arlan said. "Here comes the stage."

Lucien gulped. This was it! He'd written two letters and received one from Miss Billie (short for Wilhelmina) Jane Sneed. She described herself as twenty-four years of age, just two younger than himself, with brown hair and blue eyes. Twenty-four and unwed had him worried at first, until he saw further down in her letter that she'd been raised by her sea-captain father and traveled widely.

All that made an appealing picture. He thought it exciting and romantic, and more than once envisioned her pulling her shawl tightly about her as she stood on the windswept deck of her father's ship. He was full of questions about her adventures and where she'd traveled. That she spoke French and German also had him intrigued—he also spoke French, and Latin besides. Would she like to learn Latin, he wondered?

"Hoo boy!" Calvin said happily, smacking Lucien on the back again. Unprepared this time, he almost fell off the boardwalk as the stage pulled up.

"Steady on your feet, Luce," Arlan said with a grin. "I bet she's beautiful!"

Lucien nodded and wiped his palms on his trousers. "Yes, I'm sure she will be," he said as the driver climbed down. "She comes from the same agency as your sister-in-law Ebba."

"She does?" Calvin smiled again. "Well, don't that beat all!"

The driver came around, opened the stage door and helped the first passenger disembark. "Is that her?" Rufi asked.

"No...hey, it's Abigail!" Spencer jumped off the boardwalk and headed for the woman. "Abbey!"

"Who is this Abbey?" Rufi asked.

"She's cousin Charlotte's sister," Calvin explained. "She's prob'ly come to visit her parents."

"Billy!" Spencer shook the hand of the next passenger to disembark.

"Billy Blake used to be Spencer's deputy," Arlan explained. "Good man. He married Abbey some years back."

Lucien watched Abbey help a little boy out of the stage. He looked to be about four—Billy and Abbey's son, he presumed. He swallowed hard and wiped his hands on his trousers again.

Calvin elbowed him in the ribs. "Okay, Luce, she must be next."

The driver reached up. A purple-gloved hand appeared and took the one he offered. Those remaining on the boardwalk leaned forward in anticipation as a dark purple hat with white feathers emerged, then the rest of the woman as she disembarked the stage. Everyone took a breath as they got their first look at what had to be his mail-order bride, then stood in stunned silence.

Except Rufi. "Is she a pirate?"

Arlan put a hand over her mouth. "Hush."

"If'n she ain't, she could be," Calvin mumbled.

"Calvin!" Isabella hissed. "You are as bad as Rufi!"

Lucien's jaw dropped. She was tall…taller than even he'd had the right to hope for. And strong—not fat, but broad and…he cocked his head to one side as he studied her. Buxom, that was the word. *My, my*, he thought. This was a lot of woman! Mrs. Pettigrew had certainly delivered.

Arlan gave him a nudge. "Don't just stand there, Luce, go greet her."

"Of course." He hurried off the boardwalk to the

street. He approached her slowly, as one would a bear, then caught himself and straightened. "Miss Sneed, I presume?"

She turned to him, having been staring at the cluster of Weavers on the boardwalk. Lucien stiffened. He'd seen the eyepatch from a distance, but didn't realize until now that it was, in fact, an eyepatch—a purple one that matched her outfit, no less. She'd clearly been in some sort of adventure, or at least an accident—three thin scars poked out the top and bottom of the patch, up her forehead and down her right cheek. He batted down a frisson of anger—if someone had hurt her, he suddenly felt compelled to avenge it.

"Mr. Miller?" she said. Her voice was higher than he expected and decidedly British, but not the same British as, say, the Cookes over in Clear Creek, Oregon.

It took him a second to get his brain to work, and another for his mouth. "Yes. Lucien Miller, at your service." He bowed.

She stared at him in disbelief and stepped toward him. They were almost at eye level, and he was six-foot-two! Was she wearing heels? He watched her swallow and nod to herself, looking worried enough that he wondered if she was thinking about jumping back onto the stage.

"Your bags?" he prompted, if only to keep her there.

She blinked in dismay. "Oh yes." She looked up. "They'll have to be brought down."

"Of course." He waved at the driver. "Miss Sneed's luggage, please."

The driver took one look at her—actually, at her ample chest—then hurried to comply. Lucien did his best not to let his eyes wander in the same direction, but it was difficult. God and all His angels, she was magnificent! Tall and strong and certainly no wilting violet. At least he hoped not—he'd need the Weavers' help to carry her if she fainted. But he suspected she wasn't. She looked like the kind of warrior goddess Vikings wrote sagas about.

He'd never really bought stories of love at first sight, but now that he was experiencing it... *Oh, Madame Pettigrew—how did you know?*

"Your trunk, ma'am," the driver said as he swallowed hard and quickly set it at her feet.

"Thank you," she said, then turned back to Lucien. "Mr. Miller..."

"You must be quite tired," he said, cutting her off. He didn't know why he felt the need to interrupt—it was rude, but something deep down compelled him to do everything he could for her. She looked so frightened, this statuesque woman with a story or six to tell. She also looked like it would take a lot to frighten her, which made him wonder what the stories were.

"Er, yes, I am."

"I've arranged a room for you at the hotel," he said with a smile. He noticed her hair had red highlights when the sun hit it just so, and she had large hands (did she play the piano?). Her purple velvet jacket and white blouse were loose—for comfort, or was she trying to hide her ample bosom?—but clearly well-made and fashionable, as were her matching hat and skirt. Did she come from money? These questions and more raced through his head as he hefted her trunk onto his shoulder. "Right this way."

She didn't speak, just nodded gravely.

What could be wrong? "Are you hungry? Once you get settled, we could get something to eat."

She smiled weakly. "Of course—whatever you want."

"No, Miss Sneed—what do *you* want?"

She stared at him like a poleaxed steer for a moment. "I...er...well, I am hungry."

What was wrong with her? Dare he ask? Was she having second thoughts? And how could he broach the subject without being rude? He'd have to give that some thought. "Follow me, then."

"Of course."

Lucien forced his smile to widen as he continued toward the hotel, hoping she didn't turn tail and flee back onto the stage. For whatever reason, she looked like that's exactly what she wanted to do.

What was she doing here? Why did she ever think this would work? Billie followed the handsome (and boy, was he ever!) Lucien Miller to the small hotel down the street. The group on the boardwalk followed, staring at her like she was a carnival exhibit and happily chatting and laughing behind them. They were too far away to make out what they were saying, but close enough to hear the amusement in their voices. They were probably laughing at her.

Mrs. Pettigrew had insisted on the ridiculous hat she wore, saying it would set off the outfit perfectly. The matching eyepatch was also her idea—if she had to wear one, she might as well wear a nice one. Mrs. de la Rosa had made her several others, all just as frilly as the one she had on (the pink one trimmed in white lace was especially nauseating). How did she ever let that mad matchmaker talk her into this?

She watched Mr. Miller walking in front of her. He was a mite taller than her, thank Heaven for that! He was broad of shoulder, though nothing like the two men following her. That pair looked similar—probably related. The two women definitely were, and were exotically beautiful—French maybe, or Italian. Regardless, what was she next to them? No wonder they laughed at her.

She quelled the urge to turn and glare daggers at them. Let them laugh—she had done and could do things those two puny pansies couldn't dream of. And if she didn't scare Mr. Miller off, she would soon be married—take that!

"Would you prefer to lie down first?" Mr. Miller asked as they reached the hotel. "Then we could have a late lunch."

"No, we might as well..." She stopped. Was she jumping to conclusions? After all, shouldn't she give the man a chance to get to know her a little?

"Miss Sneed, is everything all right?"

She nodded. "Yes, I'm just tired."

"I could have them bring lunch to your room if you prefer, then join you for dinner?"

He was being so accommodating. Why didn't he just get it over with and tell her she'd never do? Someone as handsome as him should be with someone like one of the beauties behind them.

She turned and saw them approaching. The older and prettier of the two smiled. "Welcome to Nowhere! We are so happy we are in town to meet you."

Billie stared at them, unable to speak.

"Miss Sneed," Mr. Miller broke in. "May I present Mrs. Isabella Weaver and her sister Rufina Cucinotta."

Italian, then. "*Come va?*" Billie said reflexively.

Mrs. Weaver's face lit up. "*Molto bene, grazie!* You speak Italian?"

Billie nodded. "Only a little." She didn't add that most of that was foul language and imprecations, picked up from a Genoese mechanic her father had once employed. Her misgivings about getting married were only growing—with women like this in town, what chance did she have? Then again, a man usually sent off for a mail-order bride if there were no single females in the area. Isabella was obviously married, and Rufina might be too young.

The question was, would Mr. Miller keep her? She'd prepared herself for the worst, fully expecting him to reject her. So far, he'd been a perfect gentleman, but if Mrs. Weaver and her sister represented the caliber of women in Nowhere, then she was far below par. Mr. Miller would notice that soon enough, and then she'd be in a pickle.

Miss Cucinotta hadn't said anything, being too busy staring at her eyepatch. The larger of the two men gave the girl a poke with his elbow. "Arlan Weaver, ma'am. Welcome to Nowhere."

"And I'm Calvin Weaver—happy to meet ya! Mind if'n I ask where yer from? Ya got a funny accent…well, not funny like a joke, but…"

She wasn't offended. "I was born and raised in England—County Cornwall, specifically."

"That is a lovely hat," Mrs. Weaver commented. "Did it come from there?"

Billie's eyes were drawn upward. Was she making fun of it? "Thank you. And no, I got it in Denver."

"And your outfit too?" the younger said. "Or did you make it?"

"No, it was made for me."

"I knew you were a woman of taste," Mrs. Weaver said. "You let me know if you have need of a dressmaker. I make dresses for the mercantile."

"But we live a whole day from town," Rufina warned.

"True," Mrs. Weaver said with a sigh. "But Mrs. Jorgensen lives here in town—she could also make you something."

One dressmaker referring her to another? And in a small town, no less, where the competition would be keener. They were making fun of her outfit, but being subtle about it. "I'll keep that in mind."

The women smiled. "You must be tired," Mrs. Weaver said. "I remember I was when I arrived in town."

"My wife was a mail-order bride too," Calvin volunteered.

Billie felt her belly go cold. "Is that so?" She glanced at Mr. Miller, who patiently waited, her trunk still on his shoulder. "I'd best get checked in. If you will excuse us?"

"Sure thing, ma'am," Arlan said. "Hope to see you again soon."

She nodded goodbye and followed Mr. Miller inside.

The hotel wasn't anything special. There was a front lobby but no restaurant. "This is Miss Sneed," Mr. Miller told the middle-aged woman tending the front desk.

The woman smiled before her eyes locked on Billie's face. "How many nights, Lucien?"

"I'm not sure yet. Let's start with three."

The icy feeling in Billie's stomach spread to her limbs. She might as well get back on the stage—why prolong the torture? Maybe he didn't know how to tell her he'd made a mistake by sending for her in the first place. Maybe he needed time to work up to it.

Maybe he'll actually like you, a tiny voice in her mind suggested.

Billie ignored it and signed the register.

"Room seven," the woman said.

"Thank you, Mrs. Ferguson." He smiled at Billie. "Shall we?"

She preceded him up the stairs and down a hall, reading room numbers as she went. The hotel was as charming as the rest of the town looked. A small part of her wanted to see more of it, but she quickly told it to hush. No sense getting familiar with anything until she knew her fate.

"Ah, here we are." Mr. Miller unlocked the door, entered, set down her trunk and rotated his shoulder a few times. "There, that's better."

"Thank you for carrying it up for me. That was most kind."

He studied her a moment. They were standing closer than they'd ever been, close enough for Billie to notice the tiny flecks of blue in his grey eyes. "I know you're tired. Shall I call on you for dinner?"

He was so very handsome. Would he tell her over their meal, maybe after buying her return stage ticket while she rested? Was she being a pitiful fool? "Yes, thank you."

"Very well, then. Rest now, and I'll see you later." He bowed, turned and left the room, closing the door behind him.

Billie stared at the door. Maybe she should purchase her stage ticket now and save him the trouble. But at the moment, she was too tired. She lay down fully clothed, determined to at least enjoy a real bed for the three days he'd paid for. It was more than she'd expected of him.

Chapter Four

Lucien hurried downstairs, smiled at Mrs. Ferguson on his way out—and smacked right into Arlan Weaver. "Oof!"

"What's the matter, Luce, pants on fire?"

"No, of course not. Terribly sorry, Arlan—didn't see you there."

"How's Miss Sneed?"

"Fine, though tired. If you'll excuse me, I need to get some work done while she's resting."

Arlan glanced around. "Do ya have a minute to talk?"

Lucien met the big man's gaze. The Weavers were known for being loud, boisterous, even a little wild. But right now Arlan's eyes were full of concern. "What's the trouble?"

"No trouble yet, but lemme give ya a piece of advice."

Lucien stared back. "All right…"

"When yer bride tells ya how she got them scars, listen real good. They look recent. And she looks scared."

Lucien sighed. "Yes, I'd noticed that."

"Good. You and I know some folks in this town'll take one look at her and jump to all sorts of conclusions. Better ya learn the truth first so she don't suffer like Ebba did last year."

"That was Nellie Davis's doing," Lucien pointed out.

"I ain't necessarily talkin' 'bout Nellie Davis—though once she gets a gander at yer bride, Lord help us. But Mrs. Ferguson in there ain't much better sometimes."

Lucien recalled the expression on the hotel owner's face when she saw Billie, and had to agree. Who knew what she'd tell people by the time he came to fetch Miss Sneed for dinner. "I'm afraid I have to concur," he said with a sigh.

"Maybe it was just an accident," Arlan suggested. "And maybe she's scared 'cause she figures you'll reject her for it."

"I understand what you're saying. I'll hear her out."

"Does it bother you?"

"Her injury? How can I let it bother me? I could just as easily be the one with a…" He thought a moment and began to understand what Arlan was saying. "…disfiguration."

"Poor gal prob'ly ain't used to having that dis-figgeration yet," Arlan said.

Lucien raised an eyebrow. "You may be right."

"Well, just wanted to say my piece. We're headin' home in the mornin' and I ain't sure when we'll be back in town."

Lucien nodded. "Thank you, Arlan."

"Ya know what yer doin', right?"

"Whatever do you mean?"

Arlan didn't mince words. "Yer bride ain't what…

well, I ain't one to talk. When I first laid eyes on Samijo, I thought she was all wrong—'til I got to know her."

"And you're worried I'm thinking the same about Miss Sneed?"

"I'm just sayin' give her a chance. 'Specially after ya find out how she got them scars. She blind?"

"I don't know. I haven't had the chance to ask."

"And if she is?"

Lucien hadn't thought of that. But what could he do? He knew the risk he was taking in sending for a bride— you got what you got, and he was honor bound to hold up his end of the deal. "What if she is? I won't send her away for that, if that's your concern."

Arlan smiled. "Yer a good man, Lucien. She's a lucky woman to have ya."

"I'm glad you think so. I hope I live up to that observation."

"I'm sure ya will. But yer Miss Sneed ain't gonna be what folks expect."

"What they expect is none of my affair—they're not marrying her, I am. But thank you again, Arlan. I'll be careful."

"See ya stay that way," he said before walking away.

Was that a threat? No, just a warning. The Weavers weren't known for subtle diplomacy. He watched Arlan stroll toward Quinn's Mercantile, where the Weavers always stayed while in town. That meant Mrs. Quinn and Leona Riley were bound to find out about Miss Sneed before he actually married her. Would they try to draw her into one of their infamous pre-wedding frenzies? He'd heard enough stories of past debacles to be worried. What would poor Miss Sneed do—toss one of them out the store window?

Lucien shook his head. Now why would he think of that? Of course, Miss Sneed did look perfectly capable of it...

"Lucien, there you are!"

Lucien turned in time to see Leona Riley approaching. *Oh no!* Had Spencer said anything? He'd promised he wouldn't.

"I just heard the news!" she gushed. "From Mrs. Ferguson!"

Lucien glanced through the glass of the hotel doors. There was no sign of the gossiping proprietress anywhere. He hadn't been out of the building five minutes! "Oh no..."

"What was that, dear?"

"Er, nothing, Mrs. Riley. You were saying?"

"I ran into Mrs. Ferguson in the alley behind the hotel and she told me all about it!"

Lucien's eyebrows shot up. "In the alley?"

"Of course, I don't always use the front door when I visit Betsy at the mercantile. I'm practically family— I use the back when I want. And she was out back, feeding that cat of hers. But never mind about that— congratulations! It's high time we had another wedding around here."

"Indeed," he said.

"We *are* going to have a wedding, aren't we?"

His eyes narrowed. "Why wouldn't we?"

She shrugged. "Oh, no reason. It's just sometimes things don't work out." She glanced through the hotel door's window. "I hope you'll be very happy. You let me know if you need any help, won't you?"

Lucien stared at her, his brow furrowed. "I shall. What did Mrs. Ferguson tell you about my bride?"

Mrs. Riley flinched. "What? Oh, nothing. Well, I'd best take care of my business at the mercantile."

"I thought you just came from there," he pointed out.

"Heavens no—I wanted to congratulate you first."

His hands went to his hips. "Oh. So you came all the way down the alley and around the block to do it?"

"Well, I suppose I could have just as easily gone through the hotel. But I wasn't looking for you specifically, I was heading to the sheriff's office to share the news with Spencer."

Lucien's eyes flicked to Spencer's office down the street. He'd kept his secret well. But now the pressure was off the lawman. "Well, you have a nice day, Mrs. Riley."

"You too! I can't wait to meet your bride!" Off she went.

Lucien smiled, his jaw tight. "Yes, that will be quite the sight." He momentarily envisioned Miss Sneed chucking Mrs. Riley through the air, then shook his head and headed back to work.

After a fitful nap, Billie sat on the bed and stared at her unopened trunk. Should she bother to unpack, or wait and see what Mr. Miller would do? Judging from the look on the woman's face downstairs, why waste the time? She never got used to such looks, though she received them everywhere she went. Every time she looked in the mirror she felt the surgeon's needle passing through her tender flesh. She couldn't condemn anyone else for being pained at seeing her.

She stood, went to the mirror over a dresser and took off her eyepatch. The surgeon had removed the eye, leaving behind an empty socket. It was a gruesome sight even now. She wondered if she'd ever get used to it.

She replaced the eyepatch and returned to the bed. She should lie down and rest some more. It was a long way back to Denver. Could she talk Mr. Miller into sending her someplace else? Nothing said she had to return to Colorado. Wouldn't it be cheaper for him to buy her stage fare to, say, Seattle, or some obscure little town no one had ever heard of? One that wouldn't mind a one-eyed, six-foot woman with a disfigured face. A coastal town would be best—she could get work aboard a freighter or something…

Billie stretched out on the bed, her arm over her face, and willed herself not to cry. This wouldn't be the first time a man rejected her, but it would be the last. She'd find a place to settle, live out her life and be done with that stupid promise to her father. They didn't want her anyway—why should she concern herself with them?

She turned onto her side and curled into a ball. If only her father were alive. At least they'd had each other and he was fulfilling his dream. But he wasn't here and she was alone—or would be once Mr. Miller got things over with and told her they wouldn't suit. Perhaps he thought spending a few days with her would soften the rejection.

She'd been through something similar back in Cornwall…what was his name again? Oh yes, Peter Finchley. He'd come to call three times, then vanished—some story about having to visit a sick aunt in Bath. Not days later, she caught sight of him coming out of Bandy's Tavern with his friends. He'd looked right at her without batting an eye, too drunk or too cowardly to acknowledge her, before the group staggered off. Well, she was better off without the likes of him.

There were others, but Peter was the first she'd caught lying. The others had excuses of their own why they stopped calling. Most of them had probably been forced by their parents to call on her in the first place. Her father was doing well and had a bit of money—why else would they bother? But he'd spent that money on his dream of coming to America. Maybe she could keep his dream going, settle somewhere on the Pacific coast...

That accursed promise—to marry, have children, live a good life...well, she could at least attempt the third part. "I've tried, Father," she whispered. "I can't help it if the man changes his mind now that he's seen me." Once Mr. Miller sent her packing, could she consider her promise fulfilled? She'd made the effort—that had to count for something. Surely her father would understand her dilemma. She would never marry, plain and simple. Mr. Miller would be the final try.

She just wished he'd gotten it over with the moment she stepped off the stage. She'd heard enough stories on her journeys to know men were perfectly capable of abandoning women, for any reason or none. Mr. Miller hadn't done that...but Nowhere was small. The whole town would know if he left her stranded, which would be bad for his business reputation.

And the stage dropped passengers off in front of the sheriff's office—heavens, the sheriff had been standing on the boardwalk when her stage pulled up. The Blakes, the nice couple she'd traveled with, knew him and pointed him out before they disembarked. How would it have looked if he'd watched her arrive, then walked away in front of so many people? No, he'd get rid of her quietly.

Billie was sure the best she could do would be to negotiate stage and train fare to where she wanted to go. She just had to figure out where that was.

Lucien finished work and headed for the mercantile, wanting to get something nice for Miss Sneed as a welcoming gift. He'd toyed with the idea before, but after his chat with Arlan he knew he *needed* to. If Arlan saw what he saw, he had to do whatever he could to make his bride feel comfortable, accepted. Would she tell him her story over dinner, or avoid the topic? Should he bring it up? Would she be embarrassed if he did? What if her scars and injured eye were the result of some silly accident?

Better that, he mused, *than a tragedy.*

He entered the mercantile—and froze. Betsy Quinn was behind the counter! "Lucien!" she cried and clapped her hands. "I hear congratulations are in order?"

Lucien smiled weakly. "Here we go," he muttered and approached the counter, tipping his hat. "Mrs. Quinn."

"Let's get down to business," she said in a rush. "Tell me about your new bride!"

He took a deep breath. "Well, she's just arrived and is resting at the hotel."

Mrs. Quinn's eyebrows shot up. "Anything else?"

"Sorry to disappoint you, but there's nothing else to tell yet. She just got here."

"Nothing?" she said with a shake of her head. "Nothing at all?"

"I'm afraid not. But you could help me choose a gift for her—something to present to her at dinner tonight."

"Oh, how romantic!" Mrs. Quinn clasped her hands in front of her. "Let's see…jewelry? Ribbons? A lovely comb set for her hair?"

"Hmmm… I think jewelry might be a bit much. Show me the combs."

"Right over here," she said happily. She came around the counter and made a beeline for the other side of the store, where the fripperies were displayed. "I have several lovely sets."

Lucien followed her. "Yes, I see. I like this one." He picked up a silver pair of combs studded with pearls. "Are these real?"

"Afraid not. Land sakes, if they were, I wouldn't just leave them out."

"Good point." He set the combs down and looked at two others, also silver with intricate designs. He liked the simple beauty of the pearls, though, even if they were fake. "I'll take these."

"Good choice. Anything else? What color is her hair?"

"Brown, with a hint of red when the sun hits it just so…" Egads, was he waxing poetic? Well, he had quite a subject to rhapsodize about.

Mrs. Quinn smiled knowingly. "Then I should think green or purple, maybe even pink would work."

"Green, purple or pink what?"

"Ribbons, of course. A woman can never have too many ribbons." She bustled to another display and grabbed one of each color mentioned, then turned and snatched up the combs. "Well, this will make a lovely gift!"

"I quite agree. Thank you, Mrs. Quinn."

"Don't mention it." She headed for the counter. "Would you like anything else? Candy, maybe?"

"Until I know her tastes, no, thank you. I'd hate to bring her candy, then find I've chosen one she dislikes. You understand, of course."

"Of course." She went behind the counter. "You, um…know if she's blind or not? It being none of my business, you don't have to answer, but I heard she arrived wearing an eyepatch…"

And there it was. It took her longer to bring it up than he'd expected. "You heard this from Mrs. Riley, no doubt?"

Mrs. Quinn had the good grace to blush. "That and Mrs. Ferguson. Leona came to the kitchen door, but then hurried down the alley to speak with Mrs. Ferguson about something. Then she disappeared! So I went after her and that's when Mrs. Ferguson pulled me aside and…"

"You needn't explain further," he interjected. "I get the idea."

"Leona told me after Mrs. Ferguson…"

"Yes, I know," Lucien said with as much patience as he could muster. "Now could you please wrap these up?"

"Of course. I'll make them real pretty!"

Lucien rolled his eyes as she left. He knew Mrs. Riley and Mrs. Quinn weren't gossips by nature. Not as bad as Mrs. Ferguson, let alone Nellie Davis, the reigning (and convicted!) champion of the territory. Still, he didn't appreciate Mrs. Quinn's prying and he wasn't going to give her the satisfaction of telling her anything about Miss Sneed. He wasn't going to take that chance, not this time.

Mrs. Quinn placed each of his purchases in a small box, wrapped them in white paper and tied each one with blue ribbon. They were quite pretty, and he hoped Miss Sneed would be pleased. "I hope you have a nice dinner, Lucien."

"I'm sure I will." He picked up his purchases.

"Are you planning on courting this woman?"

Lucien sighed.

"I'm not trying to pry!" she blurted. "But if your bride needs help with her wedding, you know Leona and I are more than happy to lend a hand."

He grimaced. "You'll be the first to know if she does."

Mrs. Quinn beamed. "Thank you! That makes this old woman's heart sing. You know how Leona and I love helping out."

"Yes, I do." He turned to leave. "And you're not old, Mrs. Quinn. On the contrary, your willingness to help young brides prepare for their weddings is what keeps you so young." He was out the door in a flash, pledging silently to do everything possible to keep Betsy Quinn from feeling too young at Miss Sneed's expense.

Chapter Five

Billie paced. She was still wearing the same outfit, and wondered if Mr. Miller would notice when he fetched her to dinner. She thought of waiting for him in the lobby, but decided against it—she didn't feel like being stared at by people coming and going. Not that there would be, the hotel being the size it was. For all she knew, she was the only guest.

She fiddled with her hair, adjusted her eyepatch, repeated the motions. "This is ridiculous!" She paced the room, once. Why was she so nervous? She knew what was coming. Maybe knowing was what had her so fidgety. She hoped he got it over with quickly...except she still hadn't decided where to go next. She'd best make her mind up. It was the top of the dinner hour in most places...

A knock sounded on the door. Billie took a deep breath. "Right. Let's get to it, then." She crossed the room and answered it.

"Good evening," Mr. Miller said with a smile.

"Good evening," she said, more softly than she intended.

His eyes roamed over her. "I…" He shook himself. "I trust you rested?"

"Not very well, I'm afraid." She examined him in the same manner. Pity. He was such a handsome thing. All the more reason he'd be rid of her, though.

"I wasn't sure if you'd need time to dress for dinner," he said tentatively. "Of course, around here no one follows such decorum. However, as you're British I thought…"

"What I'm wearing will be fine," she broke in.

He nodded quickly. "Yes, of course. However you're comfortable." He reached into his jacket pockets. "Before we go, I'd like to give you these."

Billie stepped back in surprise when he pulled a small white box tied with blue ribbon from each pocket. Train and stage fare, maybe? *Stop it!* she silently scolded. *Besides, that will come soon enough. Maybe these are peace offerings.*

"Consider these welcome-to-Nowhere gifts. I hope you like them," he said with…was that a shy smile?… and handed them to her.

Billie took them and smiled in return, unable to help herself. For a moment he reminded her of a boy she knew back in her village of St. Ives. She'd set her cap for him, but he and his family moved away shortly after he began to take notice of her. Just her luck—the same kind she'd had ever since. "Thank you."

"You can open them now, if you like."

She could tell he wanted her to, so she obliged him. What could it hurt? At least he was giving her parting gifts. Then again, once she opened them, would the evening be over? She stepped into the hall. "Could you hold this one?"

He took one of the boxes. "I hear Hank has chicken and dumplings on the menu tonight."

"Hank?" She pulled off the ribbon and opened the first box. "Oh…"

Mr. Miller smiled. "I hope you like them. They're nothing fancy, mind, but…"

She pulled out one of two imitation-pearl-studded hair combs. "Why, Mr. Miller, these are lovely."

He smiled and sighed in relief. Was he really worried she wouldn't like them? Hmm, if he was about to suggest they wouldn't suit, of course he would. "I'm glad you think so."

She felt herself smile once again. Okay, so his gesture touched her a little. He was being as nice as he could be. "Would you mind?" She handed him the box of combs, and he gave her the unopened one in exchange. She carefully opened it and… "Ribbons!" She always did like ribbons, but didn't like spending money on them. "Thank you. These are very thoughtful gifts."

His face brightened. "Rest assured there will be more in your future."

She stiffened. How badly did he want her out of town? Did he plan to ply her with gifts all night just to soften her to the idea? He needn't bother—she'd already accepted it.

"Put those in your room and let's be off, shall we?"

Billie felt her belly twist. Did it have to be in a public place? Maybe he thought she wouldn't cause a scene if they were in public, but she wasn't going to anyway. "Yes, of course." She quickly took both boxes and ducked into her room, set them on the dresser and picked up her reticule. It was a warm night, so she wouldn't need a shawl.

When she returned to the hall, Mr. Miller offered his arm. Billie wanted to reject his gesture, but that would be rude. She might not be highborn, but she did have manners. Deep down, however, she didn't want a taste of "what could be" with this man, not even walking down the street on his arm.

They left the hotel and walked past various shops and the town mercantile. It was a lovely evening and, just as she thought, still warm. "Well," he said. "How do you like it?"

She looked around. "The town? It's…charming." Sadly, it really was. What few men strolled the boardwalks waved or tipped their hats to them—albeit with the usual curious looks she was used to. The women stared first, then offered weak smiles. At least they didn't point, whisper to each other, or frown in disapproval— they were trying to be friendly. Billie smiled and nodded in return. Whether or not they clustered and frantically whispered to each other later, she would never know— she didn't turn around.

"Ah, here we are." Mr. Miller opened the door of, so far as she could see, the only restaurant in town. Great. Once he gave her the boot, the whole town would know by morning. She knew how fast news traveled in such a hamlet. Her only consolation was that once it happened, she would never see any of these people again.

He led her to a corner table. There were few patrons, all male workingmen, and Billie's mood lightened— fewer witnesses to her humiliation. Fine—she could just take it in the cheek and move on. She smiled. She'd already "taken it in the cheek," literally, which was one reason Mr. Miller wouldn't accept her in the first place. Ah, the irony…

Mr. Miller went to the opposite side of the table and sat just as an older woman came from the kitchen. She approached their table, took one look at Billie and stopped, eyes wide, but not for long. She narrowed them and studied Billie as one would an annoying insect. Billie ignored her.

"Ah, Mrs. Davis," he said. "Two menus, please."

"I declare, what do you need a menu for, Lucien?" she said with a distinct Southern accent. "It's Thursday—chicken and dumplings night. Iced tea?" The whole time, she never took her eyes off of Billie.

"Yes, for me," he said. "Miss Sneed, what would you like to drink?"

Billie glanced between the two. Both had their eyes glued to her, but Mr. Miller's were full of compassion. Real compassion, not pity. Billie smiled. "Iced tea will be fine." She looked at the waitress. "Thank you, Mrs. Davis."

The woman's eyes skittered over her. "We haven't been properly introduced." She looked at Mr. Miller. "Well?" she demanded.

"Yes, of course, where *are* my manners?" he said. Billie did her best not to grin. "Miss Sneed, may I present Mrs. Nellie Davis." He bit his bottom lip and stiffened as if to keep from laughing. "She works for Hank, the owner of this fine establishment." Mrs. Davis glared at him.

Billie watched the exchange with interest. Of course the woman worked there—she was taking their orders, wasn't she? But why had she been so demanding when wanting to be introduced? "Not for much longer," Mrs. Davis sneered. She looked at Billie again. "What happened to you?"

Billie's mouth dropped open. She was used to getting

stared at, not outright asked. But really, why not tell her? She'd never see this boorish woman again. "If you must know, I got this defending my father from highwaymen." She pointed at her eyepatch for good measure.

Mr. Miller and the woman gasped. "What?" he said. "Great Scott, what happened?"

Billie looked away for a moment. She wasn't used to talking about her father's death, but she'd have to if she told them what happened. "My father and I were newly arrived in your county. We were traveling from New York to Philadelphia by stage when we were set upon by…well, I suppose you'd call them stagecoach robbers. They attacked the stage, killed the driver and his counterpart and…"

Mr. Miller watched her and reached his hand across the table. "You don't have to tell us if this is too hard for you."

"Quiet, Lucien, she's gotten this far!" Mrs. Davis snapped. "Go on."

Billie licked her lips and took a deep breath, surprised at her struggle for words. "They shot my father. One of them grabbed me, intent on…an outrage. He had a knife…"

Mrs. Davis gasped.

"That's enough," Mr. Miller said and stood. "Nellie, fetch us our tea. Can't you see this is upsetting her?"

"She looks fine to me," the woman said, then waggled a finger at her own eye. "Except for that."

He turned her toward the kitchen and gave her a gentle push. "Tea, Nellie. Now."

"Fine! But I want to hear the rest!" She marched to the kitchen and disappeared.

Billie glanced around the restaurant. Every eye was

on her at this point. Lovely. She put a hand to her mouth to stifle a sob and squeezed her eye shut.

"Miss Sneed!" Mr. Miller said, taking the chair next to her. "Is there anything I can do? Should I take you back to the hotel?"

"No," she managed and opened her eye. "It's just… I don't talk about it much."

He put an arm around her. "It's all right. You don't have to."

"No, I want to finish. You should know."

"I can wait. Until you're truly ready to tell me."

She looked at him, tears in her eye. *Until you're truly ready to tell me*…was he afraid her story would make him feel guilty for getting rid of her? Because it almost sounded like…like he was planning for her to be around long enough to tell? She picked up a napkin and dabbed at her good eye, then under the eyepatch. She'd lost the eye, but not its ability to weep, alas.

He in turn pulled a handkerchief from his pocket and held it out to her. "Thank you," she said.

"I had no idea," he said gently. "And Mrs. Davis is terribly rude, and an inveterate gossip besides. If you're able, you should tell her with me present—then there's a witness. She can't twist the tale that way."

"So by telling her, it will be all over town?"

"I'm afraid so," he said softly.

She used his handkerchief and handed it back.

"No, keep it." He retook his seat across the table.

Mrs. Davis returned with their iced teas and set them down. "Two chicken and dumplings?" she asked, eyes fixed on Billie again.

"Yes, please," Mr. Miller said. He looked at Billie. "Did you wish to…?"

"No," she said with a shake of her head. "Not right now."

"Fine," he said with a gentle smile, and turned back to Mrs. Davis. "Bring us two pieces of pie and coffee for dessert as well."

She took one last look at Billie, jotted down the rest of their order and left. Billie sighed in relief.

"I know," he said, worry on his face. "Who knows what she'll tell people?"

"What does it matter?" she asked. Was the man daft? If he was sending her off, why should he care? Or was he just worried about his own reputation?

"It matters to me," he said.

So, probably the latter. "I see," she said.

He still looked concerned. "Are you all right? Did they hurt you other than…?" He pointed to his own face.

"He never got the chance. I hit him with a rock while he slashed my face."

"Lord have mercy," he whispered. "But good for you, Miss Sneed, for giving them some back. Oh, you poor woman…"

"I don't want your pity, Mr. Miller."

"Pity?" Mr. Miller leaned forward and lowered his voice. "Miss Sneed, you were attacked, threatened with rape, your father murdered…trust me when I say I speak with the utmost compassion!" He sat back. "And yes, there will be those who feel pity. But people are different here in Nowhere. It's a small community and we stick together. You wouldn't be the first here to suffer tragedy and loss. Know that you're in good company on that score."

She stared at him. "And you? What have you suffered, Mr. Miller?"

* * *

What could Lucien tell her? The worst thing he'd had to suffer of late was misplacing his best tie. He'd found it, of course and was wearing it now. "Oh, I've had an easy life, really. Yes, I've lost what everyone does eventually—Death comes for us all—though I cannot say it's touched my life as directly as it has yours. I am sorry about your father, deeply so."

She swallowed and reached for her glass, nodded and took a sip. She licked her lips delicately before setting the glass down, and it almost did him in.

"I'll ask again, are you all right?" He had to know. What woman could go through so much and not be scarred? And not just her face.

"I'm fine, Mr. Miller. It was months ago."

"Months?" He stifled a chuckle of surprise. How could she be all right after mere months? "You are a brave woman." But she'd have to be to have survived. Every time she looked in the mirror, she'd be reminded of the incident and her murdered father. "Did the authorities capture them, the men who robbed the stage and killed your father?"

She'd been staring at her glass. She lifted her eyes, shook her head and returned her view to the table.

Dear Lord, the poor thing! "Are you in touch with anyone—a sheriff or deputy that can keep you abreast of what's being done?"

"There's a United States marshal who said he'd wire if there was any word. But I'm not sure he knows where I am."

Lucien shook his head. "That won't do. We'll get in contact with him first thing in the morning."

Her head came up. "What?"

"First thing in the morning," he said again. "If it were me, I'd certainly want to know. Don't you? I know these things can take time, but eventually, I'm sure those men will pay."

She stared at him in shock as Nellie brought their plates and set them on the table. "Anything else?" she asked and looked Miss Sneed over as if she couldn't stand to be so close to her. *Uh-oh,* Lucien thought. Nellie acting high and mighty was never a good sign—and he wasn't having it. "My heart rejoices that you fought off the man that gave you those scars. A few marks on the face are nothing compared to what can scar the soul. Isn't that right, Nellie—don't you think Miss Sneed's bravery should be commended?"

Miss Sneed glanced between them, goggle-eyed. Maybe he shouldn't have said anything.

But it did have the desired effect. "You fought him off?" Nellie said softly. She stared a moment longer before shocking not only Lucien, but everyone in the room and giving Miss Sneed a hug. One customer nearly choked on his coffee. "You poor, poor dear," she said before straightening. "Welcome to Nowhere. You're safe here—right, Lucien?"

"Quite right, Mrs. Davis."

Nellie nodded, as if still convincing herself. After all, it was her meddlesome gossiping that caused Ebba Weaver to almost get raped a year ago. Now the horror of such an act was sitting across the table from him. Miss Sneed's scars were a blatant reminder of the violence that existed in the world. It was obvious they'd just reminded Nellie. She retreated to the kitchen without another word.

He watched her go before reaching across the table. "Shall we pray?"

Miss Sneed, still seemingly in shock, smiled shyly. "Yes, let's." She took his hand.

Lucien smiled back, bowed his head and blessed their food.

Chapter Six

Mr. Miller walked Billie back to her hotel, escorted her up the stairs and bid her goodnight at her door. Mrs. Ferguson watched them like a hawk the entire time. *Blimey*, Billie thought, the woman takes her gossip seriously. And apparently she wasn't half the tale-bearer Nellie Davis was.

On their stroll, Lucien told her what had happened last year—for which Mrs. Davis was still performing community service at Hank's restaurant. Her tongue-wagging had caused that much trouble for one Daniel Weaver (younger brother of the two Weavers she'd met earlier) and *his* mail-order bride Ebba. It was a horrifying tale—now that she'd heard it in full, she wasn't sure she'd suffered much worse than Ebba Weaver. Still she knew hers was worse—Ebba didn't lose an eye, or a father.

But comparison wasn't going to make her life or circumstances any better. It was still just a matter of time until Mr. Miller sent her off. He might not even believe her story was true—others hadn't, had drawn their own conclusions and treated her accordingly. Badly, that is.

Billie wiped a tear away, went to the mirror and pulled off her eyepatch. Each time she looked at her reflection, she shivered. She always expected to see her old self, with her other eye, long-lashed and bright blue, looking back. Her father always told her that her eyes were her best feature, and she'd agreed, especially since she wasn't a great beauty to begin with. Now she'd lost one of those, and there was no hiding it. Plus the scars she'd wear for life.

She turned away, went to her trunk and stared at it a moment. She'd have to unpack a few things just to get ready for bed. "But nothing else," she said to herself. She put on her nightclothes, took her hair down and began to brush it out. She picked up one of the ribbons Mr. Miller had gifted her, dark blue, and held it against her brown locks. Should she wear it tomorrow? Would he be pleased if she did? Would it matter?

She tossed the ribbon onto the dresser. "Stop fooling yourself. A ribbon won't change anything." She brushed her hair harder in frustration.

When she was done, she blew out the lamp, crawled into bed and stared at the ceiling. Moonlight shone through the window, illuminating the quilt's intricate pattern. She wondered who'd made it—Mrs. Ferguson? A guest? Some woman in town? She'd never learned how to quilt, or do much of anything domestic except take care of her father. Even in that, she had help—she cooked for him now and then, but employed a cook/housemaid who took care of things the rest of the time.

While on board her father's ship, the *Nina Jane*, there wasn't much call for homemaking skills, and the ship's cook got grumpy when she went into the galley to fetch something, even if it was for her father. Mr. Scroggs was one of many that believed bringing a woman on board was bad luck. Never mind that the *Nina Jane* was built to accommodate passengers along with cargo. Sailors still didn't like the notion of a woman on board, not even as crew, which she more or less was.

She remembered the day her father sold the *Nina Jane* and most of their other belongings and booked passage for America. He was so excited to fulfill his dream—a dream soon stolen from him, and her. And now his dream for her was falling to pieces. "I'm sorry, Father. I'm so sorry…"

Tears in her eyes, Billie drifted off to sleep.

Lucien moved the vase of flowers from the dining table into the parlor and set them on the mantel. He eyed the pretty yellow bells and wild hyacinth in the evening lamplight. They were beginning to wilt—he'd have to pick more. He shook his head and returned the vase to the dining room, crossed his arms and studied them again. Did she like flowers on the table? What about the parlor? If he got up early enough, he could pick more. He wanted everything perfect when he showed Miss Sneed her future home.

Not "Miss Sneed" for long, though. "Mrs. Billie Jane Miller," he said. "Hm, I like that." He straightened and waved at the table. "And this is the dining room— how do you like it?" He shook his head. "And this is *your* dining room…" He shook it again and cleared his throat. "And here we have *our* dining room. What do you think?" He nodded, tugged at his vest and smiled in satisfaction. "There. Now for the kitchen."

Once in the kitchen, he glanced around. Everything was in order, but he really needed to bring more wood in. And…he went to a hutch, opened a drawer and pulled out a white lace tablecloth his mother had sent him last year. He'd been saving it for a special occasion, and getting married was as special as it got. He spread it over the table and smiled. "There. Very nice."

Lucien's hands went to his hips as he ran through a mental checklist of his larder. Flour, sugar, coffee, salt… he'd have to get some butter, he was out. He went back into the parlor, sat at his desk and made out a list for Mrs. Quinn at the mercantile. He'd leave it with her on his way to the bank in the morning.

But first he'd stop by the hotel and leave a message for Miss Sneed to join him for lunch. They'd need to discuss a few things before they wed—he wanted to make sure she had everything she needed to settle in. For all he knew, the poor woman was out of tooth powder. Or perfume, what about that? He didn't detect any during his time with her. Did she not wear it, or just not have any?

Details—he thrived on them, in banking and in life, and found the more he thought about his future bride, the more details he wanted. What was her favorite color? What did she like for breakfast? Heavens, did she cook? There wasn't much mentioned in her letter to him about domestic skills other than some sewing. What about gardening? Would she like the garden he'd planted? Favorite and least favored foods? Questions, so many questions.

Lucien took out another sheet of paper, dipped his pen in the inkwell and wrote down every question he could think of to ask Miss Sneed. Only then did he consider the evening done and his preparations complete.

The next morning, he got up, shaved, dressed and,

after a quick breakfast, put his list and note to Miss Sneed in his jacket pocket. He whistled as he left his little house with a nagging thought in the back of his mind—should he have made a bigger dwelling? No, two bedrooms should be enough for now. The thought made him smile, and he smiled all the way to the hotel.

"Good morning, Mr. Miller," Mrs. Ferguson said flatly as he entered.

He stopped and stared at her. She wore a disapproving look that didn't waver as he approached. "I'd like to leave a message for Miss Sneed."

"And?" She glanced at a piece of paper on the counter and scribbled something down.

He pulled the note from his pocket. "Give her this for me, won't you?"

She sighed, stopped writing and took the note from him.

Lucien wondered what had her in such a sour mood. "Is everything all right, Mrs. Ferguson?"

"Certainly, why would you think otherwise?" She glanced at the paper in front of her. "But if you must know, I'm writing my niece in Seattle a letter. She's of marriageable age, you know—I want to see if she's found any good prospects."

Lucien smiled. "I wish her well. I'm sure she'll be married in no time." He nodded goodbye. "See that Miss Sneed gets my note before nine o'clock. I'm sure she'll sleep in this morning—she's exhausted from her journey."

Mrs. Ferguson cocked her head. "Just what gave you the notion to send off for a bride from England? I thought the only fools that did that were in Clear Creek."

"I didn't. I answered an advertisement from an

agency in Denver. That Miss Sneed is English had nothing to do with it—she's simply whom they sent."

Mrs. Ferguson pressed her lips together. "Well, if you don't mind my saying so, Lucien, she seems odd to me. There's something not right about her. Surely you can do better."

Lucien arched an eyebrow as his jaw tightened. "Mrs. Ferguson, she's been through a horrible ordeal, the likes of which I will not discuss, and bears the results forever on her face. Of course there's something not right. For her, there are things that will never be right again. Remember that."

Mrs. Ferguson stood, her eyes round as platters. He hadn't scolded her exactly, just stated a fact, but from the look on her face she took it as a lecture nonetheless.

Lucien waited for a counterattack, but there was none forthcoming. Odd. "Good day, Mrs. Ferguson," he said with a tip of his hat, turned on his heel and strode out the door.

The incident stuck in his mind, though. He'd have to make sure the residents of Nowhere didn't treat Miss Sneed differently because of her injuries, physical or otherwise. He knew what damage could be wrought with the tongue, Nellie Davis being chief offender on that score. But he'd heard her daughter Charlotte had been just as vicious once. He didn't know her then and was glad of it. He much preferred Charlotte as the kind, sweet woman that took everyone under her wing.

Would Nellie ever change as her daughter had, or would she remain a cold, heartless gossip that took pleasure in stirring up trouble for others? Who knew? Her actions the night before surprised everyone, and he supposed tongues would wag about it at some point. Or not. Gossips rarely talked about the good people did, mostly the bad.

He reached the mercantile and went inside. "Good morning, Mrs. Quinn." He went straight to the counter and set down his list. "Might I pick these up after I get off work?"

"Certainly, Lucien." She looked around the store as if to make sure they were alone. "So how did supper go last night?"

He chuckled. "It was fine. And yours?"

"What? *My* supper?"

"You asked about mine."

She smiled as she caught on. "Well, it was just dandy. But can I help it if I want to make sure things are coming along for you and your mail-order bride? You'll be sure to let Leona and me know if you need our help."

He laughed. "I will. I'm having lunch with Miss Sneed today—I'll let her know." *To avoid you and Mrs. Riley until after the ceremony.*

"Thank you, Lucien, you're a dear."

He left the mercantile chuckling to himself and headed for the bank. He wondered how many people he could introduce his bride to in the coming days. And what about those outside of town—the Rileys and Johnsons, not to mention the rest of the Weavers…a shiver went up his spine. Okay, it was too soon for the Weavers. A few at a time was fine, but not the whole anarchic clan. Poor Miss Sneed might flee and not stop until she was back across the Atlantic.

He went inside the bank and straight to his office. For some reason he felt so different today. Yes, he was about to become a husband, but he hadn't foreseen the effect it would have on him. He needed someone in his life to…well, take care of. He wanted to share his shelter and food with a bride, and experience his generosity in other ways too. No, he wanted a heart to care for, protect and nurture. Miss Billie Jane Sneed was perfect.

Billie packed her nightclothes away and went to the window. It was a beautiful day with the sun shining, birds singing and a sweet smell in the air. She'd opened the window when she awoke and had kept it open ever since.

A knock on the door pulled her from her thoughts. She answered it to find a pretty woman with chestnut hair and hazel eyes, a basket on her arm and a big smile on her face. "Good morning," she said with a Southern accent. Billie remembered the waitress from the restaurant—was this a relation? "I hope you'll pardon the intrusion, but my mother told me you were staying here—not that I couldn't have figured it out on my own. You and Lucien aren't married yet…"

Billie nodded, unsure of what to say.

"I'm Charlotte Quinn. I brought you some breakfast."

"Oh, how kind." Billie stepped aside. "Won't you come in?"

"Thank you." She entered and set the basket on the dresser. "I brought muffins and bacon. The bacon's still warm, so you'll want to eat that first."

Billie smiled. "I… I don't know what to say."

"Oh, you don't have to say anything. I'm just being neighborly. I'm sure we'll see a lot of each other. My husband and his family own Quinn's Mercantile."

"I see," Billie said with a nod and pulled the napkin off the basket. The smell made her stomach growl. "Excuse me."

"Go ahead, eat. I can fetch you a cup of coffee from downstairs if you'd like. Mrs. Ferguson always keeps a pot on the stove."

"No, don't trouble yourself—you've done so much already."

"Oh, it's no trouble," she said with a wave of her hand and turned to the door. "Cream and sugar?"

Billie smiled, unable to think straight. This was the last thing she expected. "Please."

"Be right back." Charlotte breezed out the door.

Billie stared at the contents of the basket. The last major town she'd passed through, someone threw rotten fruit at her. Worse, the sight of her scarred face sent a small child screaming for his mother. She was the stuff of nightmares to some, simply ugly to others. But here… why was this woman being so kind? And what about Mr. Miller? Did he deem it a kindness to buy her gifts and food before he sent her off, or was he just trying to allay his guilt for doing so?

Speaking of which, she still needed to decide where she wanted to go.

Charlotte returned with her coffee. "Here you are, with cream and sugar." She handed her a cup and saucer. "Muffin?" she asked, pulling one from the basket.

"No, thank you, not yet. The bacon is too tempting."

"Yes, I know. I ate enough of it this morning."

Billie smiled, took a wrapped napkin from the basket and pulled out a slice. "Have you been married long?"

"A little over six years."

"Children?" She took a bite of bacon. It was heavenly.

Charlotte bowed her head. "No. For whatever reason, the good Lord hasn't seen fit to bless us with any."

Billie chewed thoughtfully, swallowed and asked, "But you want them?"

"Oh, of course. So do Mathew's parents," she added with a weak chuckle and an eye roll. "My mother-in-law reminds me often."

"Oh, I see." Billie made sure not to laugh. Though the woman was making light of the subject, she could see the pain in her eyes.

"What about you—do you want children?"

"What?" Billie said, surprised at the question. Or rather, her reaction—her heart leaped at her words. But it would never be. "One day, perhaps," she said before taking another bite of bacon.

"I'm sure Lucien does."

"Lucien? Oh." Billie smiled. "I've only called him 'Mr. Miller'." She pulled out another piece of bacon. "You must think me silly."

"Not at all—what else would you call him? You've only just met. But I hope you'll call me Charlotte."

"And you can call me Billie."

"Billie? I haven't heard a woman go by that name before. I like it."

"Billie Jane, to be exact. My father called me Jane, but also Billie a lot."

"And you prefer Billie?"

"Yes."

"Very well, Billie it is," she said. "Mind if I share a muffin with you?"

Billie smiled again. "No, not at all."

Charlotte smiled back before taking a muffin from the basket along with a butter knife and cut it in two. "It's nice to make a new friend. Wait until you meet some of the other ladies in town—I'm sure you'll like them."

Billie took the half she offered and put it on a napkin. What else could she do? For all she knew she'd be leaving on the afternoon stage. Pity—she was beginning to like Charlotte Quinn.

Chapter Seven

The two women were laughing at Charlotte's tales of her husband and family, especially her rowdy cousins the Weavers, when there was another knock at the door. Billie opened it to find Mrs. Ferguson. "Yes?"

The hotelier handed her a folded note. "Mr. Miller left this for you earlier."

"Oh?" She did her best to remain calm. He sent her a note? Is this how he would end it?

Mrs. Ferguson flicked a hand across her skirt. "He wants you to meet him at Hank's for lunch."

Charlotte left the chair she'd been using and joined Billie at the door. "Why didn't you have me bring that up when I brought the coffee?"

"Mr. Miller told me to deliver it at nine," she said, patting her hair.

"And why tell her what's *in* the note before she's had a chance to read it?" Charlotte added, crossing her arms.

"Can I help it if it unfolded?" Mrs. Ferguson huffed. She turned to leave and stopped. "Is your mother working at Hank's today?"

"Yes, of course." Charlotte let her arms fall to her sides.

Billie noticed Charlotte had a suspicious gleam in her eye. Did she not trust Mrs. Ferguson either? Billie didn't, not after she'd read a note intended for a patron. Blimey, she still hadn't read it herself.

"I'll be downstairs if anyone needs me," Mrs. Ferguson said, feigning innocence. Chin up, she turned and strode down the hall to the stairs.

"I declare," Charlotte said. "The sooner you marry Lucien, the better."

Billie thought of a comment about gossips, remembered Mrs. Davis was Charlotte's mother, and suppressed it. What she couldn't recall was whether or not Charlotte was a gossip as well.

"Were you going to say something?" Charlotte asked.

Billie shook her head.

"Maybe you ought to read that note and see if Mrs. Ferguson remembered it right. Gossips aren't known for their accuracy."

Billie did. "No, she recalled this one correctly—word for word." She handed it to Charlotte.

"There was a time I could read a letter in seconds and remember all the good stuff." Charlotte shook her head and handed it back. "I'm glad those days are behind me."

Billie wasn't surprised. Aside from her own assessment, Mr. Miller had spoken of Charlotte last night, more complimentarily than of her mother. Was that conversation considered gossip, or just recollection? "Really?"

"Oh, let me tell you, I could slander with the best of

them—the best, of course, being my mother. I'm sure she served your dinner last night."

"Yes, I had the pleasure of meeting her," Billie said carefully. She didn't want to offend Charlotte, nor tell her of her mother's behavior earlier in the evening. "But she gave me a fairly warm welcome."

Charlotte's expression changed to panic. "Heaven help us, what did she do?"

"She gave me a hug."

Charlotte's jaw dropped. "*My* mother gave you a hug?" She walked to the other side of the room and back. "Are we talking about the same woman?"

"I believe so. From your reaction and that of the patrons in the restaurant last night, I take it that isn't normal behavior?"

"I should say not," Charlotte said, hands on hips. "Will wonders never cease? I'm surprised...no, downright *elated* to hear she did such a thing." She went to Billie and took her by the hand. "Was Hank's crowded last night?"

"No, just Mr. Miller and myself and a few gentlemen at other tables."

"Good. At least a few people saw her do the right thing. Heaven knows if her time at Hank's has done much good."

Billie went to the dresser and picked up her half of the muffin. "Mr. Miller told me what happened last year. I hope you don't mind his informing me." She sat in a nearby chair, broke off a piece and put it in her mouth.

Charlotte joined her and sat on the settee. "Not at all. It's not as if the whole town doesn't know. Besides, her sentence is almost up."

Billie swallowed and studied Charlotte for a moment. She was pretty and kind-looking and seemingly wouldn't hurt a fly. It was hard to believe she'd been such a harpy years ago. "Is your mother really that bad?"

"My father says that if Mother had fought in the War Between the States, the Confederacy would've won. She would've *harangued* the Union to defeat."

Billie covered her mouth to stifle a chuckle.

"I imagine you think I'm joking, but where do you think I learned? I suspect the only thing that saved me from turning out like her, was that I hadn't been doing those things as long as she has. She's got quite a few years on me."

"She knows how I got this." Billie pointed at her face.

"She does?" Charlotte said in shock. "Tarnation, I hope you don't mind that being spread all over town."

"She got the truth, so if that's what she spreads, I can cope with it."

Charlotte stared at her and shook her head. "You are much braver than I. But then, I know my mother better than you—and I understand how she thinks better than anyone except maybe Father."

"I haven't offended you, have I?" Billie didn't know why she asked, other than not wanting to spoil the rest of their visit.

"Of course not. But enough about my mother. Have you and Lucien set a date? Matthew and I would love to attend your wedding."

Billie smiled. "I'd… I'd like that, but…"

"There are no buts. I want us to be friends, and I think attending your wedding is a good start, don't you?" She got up, went to the basket, took out the rest of the muffins and set them on the table. "I'm afraid I do have to get back to the mercantile. You'll let me know when the big day is?"

Billie felt the hot sting of tears. "Of course." Thank Heaven her voice didn't crack.

"Wonderful! My sister Abigail is in town and I know she'll want to meet you." Charlotte smiled. "This might sound odd, but I just *love* your eyepatch."

"What?" Billie said in surprise. "You...*like* my eye-patch?"

"It matches your traveling outfit perfectly. I mean, if you have to wear one, why not be fashionable about it?"

Billie couldn't help but grin—it was almost word-for-word what Mrs. Pettigrew had said. "When the dressmaker made them, I thought they were silly."

"Them? You mean you have more?"

"Yes, several."

"I can't wait to see them. But not until you meet my sister Abigail—Abbey for short. She loves to sew." She peered at the eyepatch. "I must say, that was a good idea. It says you're not ashamed to have people look at you. Like I said, you're much braver than I." She turned and headed for the door. "Come visit me at the mercantile when you get a chance—we have some lovely things. I'm sure I'll see you soon." She opened the door and stepped into the hall.

Billie smiled and nodded as she went to the door and closed it. Again, she had nothing to say. Okay, she had quite a few things, all of which would bring her nothing but disappointment if voiced. Like, "yes, I know we can be friends" and "I would love to come to your store and see what you carry. I'm sure everything's lovely, just as you are" and maybe "thank you for asking to attend my wedding." But she still didn't think she would be in Nowhere long enough.

Poor Charlotte. The woman seemed genuinely interested in her and sincere about wanting to be friends. Maybe she needed a friend to fill the void caused by not having children. Yes, that was probably it.

She straightened her room, ate another muffin and finished her coffee. She debated whether or not to take the cup and saucer downstairs to Mrs. Ferguson's kitchen, but decided she'd wait until it was time to meet Lucien.

She gasped. "Oh, for Heaven's sake," she said aloud, "don't start calling him by his first name!" What was the point?

Billie opened her trunk and pulled out a book she'd picked up in New York City, deciding to read for a bit. She had several hours to herself and needed to fill them. Maybe she could go to the mercantile to visit Charlotte, see what wares they carried. She'd need a few things before she left town—best get them now while she had the money. But first things first—she settled into a chair, opened *Two Years Before the Mast* and began to read.

She soon dozed off, and when she awoke it was to a headache and stiff neck. No matter, she was used to those. She got them often after her injury. Thankfully, they were less frequent recently—a good sign, or so a doctor had told her.

She fixed her hair, took up her reticule and the cup and saucer and left, planning to return the dishes and go to the mercantile. What did she have to lose by spending a little more time with Charlotte? Besides, she wanted to meet her husband Matthew—he sounded like someone Father would have liked.

"Rather early for lunch, isn't it?" Mrs. Ferguson said from behind the front desk.

Billie didn't like her accusatory tone. "Charlotte invited me to visit her family's mercantile."

"Oh yes, Quinn's has a nice selection of goods."

Billie set the cup and saucer on the counter. "I brought these down for you. Would you like me to put them in the kitchen?" She glanced behind the woman—where *was* the kitchen in this place?

"No, I'll take them back myself." Mrs. Ferguson scooted them to her side of the counter. "So you're to marry Mr. Miller."

Billie's good eyebrow went up in curiosity. Of course she was there to marry Mr. Miller—by now the whole town probably knew. "Yes…"

"Well, if you don't mind my saying, I…no. No, I can't." Mrs. Ferguson reached for a stack of papers and tapped them against the counter to straighten them.

Billie knew she shouldn't, but did anyway. "You can't what?"

"Isn't my business. I told my Howard I wouldn't poke my nose into anyone else's business ever again."

"Howard?"

"My husband. Dead these five years now, God rest his soul. That man was my life."

A pang of guilt hit Billie. "I'm sorry for your loss. I know what it's like to lose someone you love."

Mrs. Ferguson's eyebrows rose with interest. "Do tell?"

"My father. Just a few months ago."

"Oh, you poor dear. Is that why you became a mail-order bride?"

Billie couldn't tell if she was serious or simply digging for information. But she'd already told Mrs. Davis most of her story. "It was my father's dying wish that I marry." There, now the woman had information no one else did. If it got spread all over town, she'd know the source.

"His dying wish!" Mrs. Ferguson said in surprise. "So you're telling me the only reason you're marrying our Lucien is because it was your father's last request?"

Billie saw where this was going. "Not exactly what I said."

"Oh yes, it was," Mrs. Ferguson said with a gleam in her eye.

Oh, for Heaven's sake, Billie thought. "I have other reasons for becoming a mail-order bride as well. That's just one of them." There, that should fix it.

The older woman frowned in indecision. "Well, I should hope so. We're very fond of Lucien around here and don't want to see him hornswoggled."

"Horn…swoggled?"

"Oh, I keep forgetting you're not from this country. Is that part of why you're getting married, because you can't afford to go back to England?"

Billie had had enough. She was tempted to remove her eyepatch and give Mrs. Ferguson the shock of her life. But she resisted. "No, no. If I wanted to go back to England, I'd have done so."

Mrs. Ferguson looked her up and down. "Well, I can certainly see why you'd want to stay."

Billie shook her head, deciding she didn't want to know what *that* meant. "Have a good day, Mrs. Ferguson." She left the hotel without looking back. Let the woman think what she wanted. Why should she care, when she was leaving soon anyway?

She walked down the street to the mercantile and went inside. "Oh my," she whispered as she saw the array of goods. She hadn't expected so much stock in a small-town frontier shoppe. There were barrels of candy lined up opposite long tables to create multiple aisles, ready-made clothes on racks and tables on the far side of the room, sugar and flour and coffee and other staple foodstuffs, an entire bookshelf full of volumes and pamphlets, and equipment for farming, ranching, mining and many other occupations.

But what she noticed most was the homey feel of the place, something she'd never encountered in any general store in England or America. It made her want to curl up in a comfortable chair (and there were a couple, in a corner by the bookshelf) and live there for a while.

"Billie!" Charlotte called from behind the counter. "You came!"

"Of course I did. You made it sound so nice." She went to the counter and smiled at the older woman standing next to Charlotte. "Hello."

"Billie, this is my mother-in-law Betsy Quinn."

Mrs. Quinn rushed around the counter and took Billie by the hands. "Land sakes, just look at you! How marvelous!"

Billie's eye went wide. What was so marvelous about being the size of a tugboat, with a scarred face and an eyepatch?

"Now, Charlotte, ivory or what?" Mrs. Quinn said as she tapped her chin with a finger.

"Oh no, not now," Charlotte said. "That's not why she's here."

Mrs. Quinn's brow furrowed. "She's not? But it's the

perfect time." She leaned toward the counter. "For once I can dress a bride myself, without Leona horning in…"

Charlotte put a hand over her mouth to stifle a laugh. "Yes, I understand that," she said into the hand, then lowered it. "But Billie came to see the mercantile…*not* have you help with anything."

Mrs. Quinn turned to Billie with an acute look of disappointment. "Aw shucks, I was so looking forward to helping you with your wedding. And with your lovely brown hair and blue eyes…well, eye. I think you'd look stunning in white…"

"Mother Quinn," Charlotte said, rolling her eyes. "Please?"

Billie glanced between the two. *She* knew there wasn't going to be any wedding, but they didn't. What to do? She took a step back for safety's sake. "Who is Leona?"

"Oh, she's my dearest friend," Mrs. Quinn said with a clap of her hands. "We've been dressing brides together for years! But we don't always agree."

Billie saw the manic look in her eyes. Oh dear. "Is that so?"

"Oh yes!" Mrs. Quinn said with a wide grin. "There's not a bride that can slip by us!"

"I believe that," Billie muttered.

Mrs. Quinn smiled proudly and returned to her place behind the counter. "What would you like to see, dear? White lace, perhaps?"

"Mother Quinn," Charlotte warned. "Will you stop?"

"I know I need to," she whined, slapping the counter. "But I just can't help myself."

Charlotte glared at her. "Try." She went around the counter to Billie. "This way, we have some lovely new perfumes in. You might find some you like. And if you can't buy anything yourself, I know Lucien will buy it for you."

Billie giggled, unable to help it as Charlotte took her arm and led her to the other side of the store. Charlotte and her mother-in-law's antics were making it harder and harder for her to come to grips with leaving. She liked these people and wanted to get to know them better. But as she let Charlotte tug her along to the perfumes and tried them, she realized that for the first time since her father's death, she was having fun. And that was better than nothing.

Chapter Eight

Billie found it hard to leave the mercantile. Charlotte Quinn was engaging, fun, sophisticated, well-read, ladylike—everything Billie wished she could be but wasn't, even before her injury. It was hard to believe this was the daughter of Nellie Davis, the town's worst gossip. Then again, she'd confessed she hadn't always been so nice—best remember that, just in case. But she liked Charlotte a lot, despite what Mr. Miller had told her.

Oh dear—Mr. Miller, she thought as she set her purchases on the dresser. They were meeting for lunch in an hour. She'd spent longer than expected with Charlotte, having too good a time to pull away. Charlotte must have enjoyed it too—she'd invited Billie to tea that afternoon. Billie had briefly met Charlotte's sister Abigail when she arrived, but looked forward to spending more time with her. According to Charlotte, she was an exceptional seamstress.

She wondered if Abbey had also been different years ago. Had she gossiped? Hurt people? Caused a stir wherever she went? But honestly, why was she worrying about other people's pasts? Perhaps a nice relaxing tea was what she needed. She just hoped Mr. Miller didn't send her off on the afternoon stage—it would be a pity to miss it.

Billie packed her purchases into her trunk in preparation for her inevitable departure. If she could spend another night, she'd leave Nowhere happy and even somewhat fulfilled. Her hope now was to find the same happiness she had today someplace else like… Seattle. Yes, that was an idea. It was a large enough city to provide work *and* cheap accommodations. Plus, other than San Francisco, it was the only seaport she'd heard of within a thousand miles.

She read until it was time to meet Mr. Miller for lunch. When she left the hotel Mrs. Ferguson was nowhere in sight. Which was a mercy—who knew what her comings and goings would conjure in the woman's mind. She reached Hank's Restaurant, but didn't see Mr. Miller. It was noon—where was he? "Oh, goodness, was I supposed to meet him at the hotel?" she muttered. Or worse, was he not going to show?

"Well, hello again!"

Billie turned to see Nellie Davis, coffeepot in hand. "Hello. How are you?"

"I've been better. Of course, I was always better before I had to work here, but that's a story I don't want to bore you with. Coffee?"

"I was supposed to meet Mr. Miller, but perhaps I was supposed to meet him at the hotel."

"Never mind that—have a seat and I'll pour you a cup." Nellie waved toward a chair, and Billie shrugged and took it. Nellie poured her some coffee, went to the kitchen and returned with another cup, which she filled. "There—now his coffee's waiting for him when he gets here."

"Thank you, Mrs. Davis, that was very thoughtful," Billie said.

"Well, it's just good manners. I suppose if I were hosting in my home I would do the same."

"Do you work here all day?"

"Depends on the day. I'm off in a few hours—I'm not working the supper shift today."

"That's good to hear. I'm, um, having tea with your daughter later this afternoon."

"You are? Then we'll be having tea together. Charlotte came by here earlier and invited me."

Billie wasn't sure if this was good or bad. But manners… "I look forward to it."

"And I'm sure Mr. Miller is looking forward to lunch with you," she said, tossing her head at the door. "There's your beau now."

Billie turned as Mr. Miller approached them with a smile. "Hello. Sorry I'm late—I went to the hotel to get you."

"I'm sure all's forgiven, Lucien," Nellie drawled. "I just poured your coffee. Special today's beef stew." She headed back to the kitchen.

Mr. Miller cringed as he sat. "I'm ordering a ham sandwich. Hank's stew is too heavy for me."

"Oh?" Billie glanced at the kitchen and back. "Then I think I'll have the same."

"Wise decision," he said with a chuckle. "So how was your morning?"

Billie saw his bright eyes and cheerful demeanor, and hoped he wasn't so happy *because* she was leaving. "It was fine," she said as her eye drifted to the table. She took a sip of coffee to battle the tears.

"Mine was busy—papers, papers, papers. As always. Any plans this afternoon?"

"Charlotte Quinn invited me to tea," she said, eye still on the table.

"Tea? That's wonderful—you're making friends already." He took a sip of coffee, set it down and smiled even wider.

"What is it?" she asked, catching the flicker of anticipation in his eyes.

"Well…" He leaned forward. "After your tea, how would you like to see our house?"

Billie froze. "House?" *Our?!*

"Yes…is something the matter?" he asked, concerned. "I thought you might like to see it. If you're worried about a chaperone, we can ask Charlotte or someone else to accompany us. You needn't worry about that."

Billie could only stare. "Why…why would you want to show me your house?"

He looked baffled. "Excuse me…you're asking *why*? Because it's where you're going to live, of course."

Billie's chest tightened. What was he doing, toying with her like this?

He leaned forward again. "Miss Sneed… Billie? What's the matter?"

Good heavens, he was using her Christian name! "I… It's just… I didn't expect…"

"You didn't expect what?"

She shook her head. "Never mind. If you'd like me to see your house, that's fine."

His face twisted with confusion. "I don't understand. What's…?"

"Have you made up your minds?" Nellie interrupted as she approached their table.

Mr. Miller's eyes flicked between the two women. "Um, ham sandwich, please. And what do you mean, never mind?"

"Never mind?" Nellie said. "Never mind what?"

"He was speaking to me, Mrs. Davis," Billie said.

"Oh, my mistake. Do you know what you want to order?"

"I'll have the same, please," Billie said. "And an iced tea."

"Right, iced tea. Lucien?"

"I'll stick with the coffee." He waved her away, his eyes locked on Billie's. "Now what's this all about?"

"It's about lunch." Nellie grumbled before stomping off.

Billie smiled at the quip. Gossipmonger she might be, but Billie was beginning to like her spunk. Not that it mattered. "I assure you, Mr. Miller, it's nothing."

"If you say so," he replied, sounding like he didn't buy it for a second. He sat back in his chair. "And please, call me Lucien."

Lucien. She tried the word out in her mind first. "All right, Lucien."

"And is it all right to call you Billie?"

"Of course. It's what I've gone by for years."

"Yes, of course." He blushed slightly, which for some reason made him more attractive. He fiddled with his napkin and put it on his lap. "Billie, I wish you'd tell me what's wrong."

"It's nothing, really." Except that he wanted to show

her his house—and called it "our house"! Why would he say that? It made no sense.

"If you're sure." He studied her intently, clearly not sure at all.

"I'm sure." She folded her hands in front of her stomach, which was flip-flopping all over. He was so bloody handsome—far too handsome for the likes of her. And he was making her nervous, leading her on like this. She kept waiting for him to tell her this wouldn't work, that she had to go, that he was *so* sorry they didn't suit… what was taking him so long?

Even now he just nodded, accepting her answer. "Then perhaps it's better you spend the afternoon with Charlotte. I want you to feel welcome here. I don't want to rush you or make you uncomfortable."

"Thank you, that's very considerate," she replied, as in the back of her mind she was screaming. *Rush it, already! Just say it—don't leave me twisting in the wind like this, just give me the shove!*

"You've had a long journey and one night of sleep isn't enough to make up for it. Forgive me. I don't want to push you into anything too soon. I know I wouldn't want to be…"

Oh, enough was enough! She just wished he'd get it over with, and if he wouldn't do it on his own, she was more than happy at this point to nudge him toward it. "I suppose we should decide on a date and time." He could interpret it as "a date and time to send her away" or "a date and time to wed"—either way, it would hopefully make him act.

No such luck. "Yes, of course. If you like, we can do it together, or I can make the arrangements. Whichever you prefer." That smile again.

She bit her lip to keep the tears back. "I'll…let you handle things." She almost choked on the words. Thankfully, Nellie brought their sandwiches and her iced tea, giving her something else to look at. It wasn't bad enough he was packing her off—he was elated at the prospect *and* more than happy to prolong her agony by stretching it out before actually saying the words.

Not waiting for him to say the blessing, Billie picked up her sandwich, bit into it and willed herself not to cry.

Abigail Blake's little boy was adorable. As was Abbey, as she preferred to be called. She was as good a seamstress as Charlotte had told her—Billie couldn't take her eyes off the woman's day dress.

"When is Mother getting here?" Abbey asked as Charlotte poured her a cup of tea. They were in the parlor of the Quinns' flat behind the mercantile. Billie found their quarters charming, and had visions of opening a shop in Seattle and living on the premises. But what kind of shop? She couldn't sew like Abbey or Isabella Weaver, so dressmaking was out. She didn't cook well enough to open a bakery or restaurant. Perhaps a chandler's, supplying ships—but first she'd need starting capital…

"Maybe she had to work late at Hank's," Charlotte suggested, filling Billie's cup. "Sugar?"

"Please," Billie said.

"I hope you don't mind my saying," Abbey said, "but I simply adore your eyepatch. It matches your outfit perfectly."

Billie was still wearing her purple traveling outfit. As some point she really should change, but that would mean unpacking and repacking. "Thank you. The dressmaker thought it would be a good idea to make everything match."

"And she has more of them, Abbey," Charlotte said. "Don't you, Billie?"

"Yes, several—each matching an outfit." Egads, this was awkward.

"How wonderful. What a marvelous idea." Abbey took a sip of her tea and studied Billie.

Billie sighed. She might as well get it over with. "I was attacked." She waved at her face. "That's why the scars. And I lost my eye."

Abbey gasped, a hand to her chest. "You poor darling. Does it still hurt?"

"I just get headaches sometimes."

Just then, Nellie entered the parlor with Mrs. Quinn. "There she is, our new bride!"

"Yes, we've met," Mrs. Quinn added. "Haven't we, Miss Sneed?"

"Indeed." Billie took another sip. She watched the two matrons seat themselves and fought a pang of loneliness. She often dreamed of having tea with women who accepted her for who she was, long before she lost her father, her eye and what looks she had. Now here she was, doing just that, feeling almost like an equal with them…and knowing it wouldn't last. She fought against a sigh. Well, she'd better enjoy it while she had the chance.

"Davey, come see your Grandmama." Nellie held her arms out to Abbey's little boy.

"Granny!" Davey ran to her, laughing as Nellie scooped him onto her lap. Mrs. Quinn watched the pair with envy, and Billie's heart went out to her. What if Charlotte could never have children? It was obvious Betsy Quinn wanted grandchildren, but sometimes things didn't work out as people hoped.

She set the thought aside—what business was it of hers? She needed to worry about finding a job in Seattle once she got there, and enjoying the company of the ladies around her while she could. "Have you all lived here a long time?" she asked to change the subject.

"My goodness, yes," Betsy said. "Seems like we've been here forever. Matthew was raised here."

"We've been here a long time as well," Nellie said. "Though not as long as Betsy and her family."

"Are most of the families here original settlers?" Billie asked.

"Most of them, yes," Betsy said. "The newer folks in town are mainly women—mail-order brides like you."

Billie lowered her head. "Really?"

"Except for that brood of Calvin Weaver's," Nellie said archly.

"Mother," Charlotte warned.

"Don't you 'mother' me. It's a wonder I've survived the year!"

"*Mother...*"

"Now, ladies," Betsy said. "Let's forget last year and enjoy our tea. It's too bad Leona couldn't join us."

"Leona?" Billie said. Wasn't she Mrs. Quinn's partner in nuptial crime? Or her rival? It was rather unclear.

"Thank heavens she's not," Nellie drawled and gave Billie a pointed look.

Charlotte and Abigail giggled. "You remember me telling you about them earlier, don't you?" Charlotte asked Billie.

"Yes, I seem to recall," Billie said and smiled.

Nellie rolled her eyes. "The two of you didn't overdo

it with Abbey or Charlotte, did you? Mercy me, I can't remember."

"No," Betsy said. "Nothing like what we did to Summer and Elle Riley! Remember that, Charlotte?"

"Must I?" she said flatly, then leaned toward Billie. "Back then I was such a shrew," she sighed.

Nellie stared at the tea tray. "You still weren't as bad as I was."

Everyone looked at Nellie in shock—except Billie, who was watching the others' reactions. Just how bad had Nellie been?

Nellie looked at each of them in turn. "Yes, I've done some thinking while working at Hank's," she said, as if that explained everything. Maybe it did.

Charlotte touched her mother's hand. "We were both terrible back then. Some of the things I said to Summer and Elle were unforgivable."

"Yes, but the Rileys *did* forgive you. I'm not sure they'll ever forgive me, or that anyone in this town will." She took a quick sip of tea. "Might just be my burden to bear."

Billie looked from one face to the other. "Forgiveness is difficult." She took a sip, hiding behind the rim of her cup in embarrassment—she wasn't sure why she'd said that. It just popped out.

Nellie slowly nodded. "You're right, child, it is. And more for some than others. I know how hard it is for me."

Abbey smiled at her. "Mother, people *will* forgive you. You just have to be patient."

"And it doesn't hurt to ask for it," Charlotte tacked on.

Nellie's eyes flashed. "I don't think I can do that. I'm not like you."

Betsy looked at her. "Nellie?"

"What?"

"*I* forgive you."

Once again, the others stared in shock. Billie sensed something major was taking place. She took another sip of her tea and continued to watch.

"Betsy…" Nellie whispered. "You do?"

Betsy nodded. "What you did last year to Daniel and Ebba was downright scandalous. And in our mercantile, no less. But I forgive you for stealing that letter, and I hope others will too." She looked at Charlotte.

"Oh, Mother, you know I forgive you. Matthew has too."

"He's never said anything to me," Nellie stated, looking put out.

"You've never asked him."

"I don't know if I can," Nellie said. "Pride's a powerful thing."

Billie watched and listened, a lump in her throat that the tea wouldn't shift. Could she forgive the man who killed her father and blinded her? Could she forgive him for what he'd been about to do to her—what the whole gang of robbers would have done, given half the chance? Thank Heaven they never got it, but if they had…

Nellie reached for a cookie. "So tell us, Miss Sneed—when are you getting married?"

Chapter Nine

Billie began to cough, though she hadn't taken another sip. Abbey patted her on the back. "Are you all right?"

"Yes…*cough*… I'm sure I shall be."

"I declare," Nellie said. "I hope the mention of marriage doesn't do this to you all the time."

"Mother!" Charlotte said with a roll of her eyes.

"I did say I wouldn't change overnight, didn't I?"

"That's beside the point." Charlotte poured Billie more tea. "Here, drink this."

Billie sipped slowly. Maybe if she prayed hard enough, they'd change the subject.

But that wasn't about to happen. "Do you have a wedding dress?" Abbey asked.

Billie tried to clear her throat, with mixed results. "There wasn't time."

"Did you hear that, Charlotte?" Betsy exclaimed. "This poor dear needs a wedding dress!"

"Could we perhaps let *her* decide what she needs?" Charlotte groaned, reaching for a cookie.

"Betsy, control yourself," Nellie said. "Leave the poor girl be. If she wants a dress, then I'm sure she'll have you and Leona, or Abbey and Charlotte, or whomever else wants to get in on it help. Right now, let the poor thing breathe."

Billie nodded vigorously in agreement. She took a deep breath and let it out slowly. Thank Heaven that was over. She didn't dare tell them what was really going on. If they found out Mr. Miller was about to purchase her stage fare out of town, what would they think then? Nellie already had enough ammunition to damage Billie's reputation if she chose. Not that others hadn't tried, and like Nellie she'd never have to see them again. Let them think she was ruined. She and the Lord knew the truth.

"My mother's right," Abbey said, breaking into her thoughts. "Any one of us would be happy to help you make a dress, if that's what you want."

Billie held her cup in both hands, enjoying the warmth. *It would be nice to have an actual wedding dress*, she mused, *if I was actually getting married*. "I'll give it some thought," she replied, stalling for time. "Were you married here?"

"Yes, and what a day that was!" Abbey laughed.

Nellie put a hand to her temple. "I try not to think about it."

"Oh, Mother!" Charlotte turned to Billie. "It was quite a day—it changed my life as well as Abbey's."

Billie wasn't sure if she should ask Charlotte to explain.

Betsy Quinn resolved it for her. "Elle and Spencer Riley were supposed to be getting married, but then Abbey and Billy got married instead. And the whole event…well, kind of shocked Charlotte out of some bad habits, I think."

"Well put, Mother Quinn," Charlotte replied with some amusement. "And just in time for Matthew to return to town—though that led to a tangle of its own."

Betsy nodded. "We'll have to tell you all about it sometime, Miss Sneed. Right now I need to go mind the store so Matthew can take a break." She set her cup down and stood. "Coming, Nellie, or did you want to visit a while longer?"

"I think I'll visit," Nellie said. "It's not often I get to have tea with the ladies."

"Very well. I'll go fill your list." Betsy headed for the storefront as Charlotte began to refill everyone's cup.

Except for Billie's—she was sipping hers slowly in case someone brought up Mr. Miller again. She'd have to be careful not to be taken by surprise and spew tea all over the cookies. How embarrassing would that be?

"Have you seen Lucien's house yet?" Nellie asked.

Billie set down her cup so as to not risk an accident. "No, not yet."

"He's quite proud of it," Nellie informed her. "Oversaw the building of it himself."

Charlotte nodded. "I helped him pick out a few things, though only a few. Lucien Miller isn't just an educated man, but he also has very good taste."

"Is it true he comes from back east?" Abbey asked.

"Connecticut," Nellie said. "If you ask me, he's quite a catch. You're a lucky woman, Miss Sneed."

"Why, Mother, what a nice thing to say," Abbey said. "And I have to agree—educated, gentlemanly and very handsome."

Billie smiled weakly and looked away. He was all that and more. And none of them were saying it, but they had to be thinking: *how could a man as gorgeous as Lucien Miller marry a monstrosity like Billie Sneed?*

"Cookie?" Charlotte asked and offered the plate to Billie.

"Thank you, but… I'm rather tired. You don't mind if I return to the hotel, do you?"

The three women exchanged a look. "No, not at all," Charlotte said.

"My husband and I are in town for a couple of weeks," Abbey said. "You'll let me know if you'd like some help with your dress?"

Billie's smile was heartfelt. These women were so nice, even Mrs. Davis, the reputed harbinger of ruined reputations. The more time she spent with them, the harder it would be to leave. "Yes, I'll let you know." She put her cup and saucer down, picked up her reticule and stood.

"I really wish you could stay and visit a little longer," Charlotte replied. "But we understand you being tired and all. Let us know as soon as you and Lucien have a date—we'd love to attend your wedding."

Billie felt a lump of guilt settle in her gut. "Certainly."

Abbey and Nellie also prepared to leave, and the women escorted Billie to the storefront, said their goodbyes and happily waved as she departed.

Once outside Billie exhaled. She didn't dare spend any more time with them—it would only make leaving harder. If she was smart, she'd return to the hotel and stay there. The only reason to see Lucien Miller at this point was to get her stage and train tickets from him. With a heavy heart, she took one last look at the mercantile before walking away.

"How about Saturday?" Mabel Lewis, the preacher's wife, asked.

"Yes, that's fine," Lucien said happily. He put on his hat and stood. "Ten o'clock?"

"Yes indeedy." She jotted it down in a little book and got up from the desk. "Lucien, I know it's none of my business, but are you sure this is what you want?"

"Mabel, I sent away for a mail-order bride in order to marry her. That's how it works."

"Yes, but…" She stopped and fidgeted.

Lucien's eyes narrowed in suspicion. "But what?"

She made a face. "Well… I hear that the woman isn't exactly, erm…" She made a circular motion with her hand. "…what one would expect." She folded her hands primly in front of her and gave him a motherly look.

He knew she was only looking out for him, unlike some others who'd voiced their opinions. But he still didn't like the insinuation. He crossed his arms. "Are you referring to her eyepatch, her scars or her size?"

Mabel's eyes widened. "Just how big is she?"

"Smaller than I am." Now he was curious as to what the gossips—specifically, Mrs. Ferguson—were saying. "What have you heard?"

Mabel looked away and let her hands fall to her sides. "Oh, I haven't heard a thing."

"Mabel, you're a rotten liar."

"Lack of practice, what with being the preacher's wife." She met his gaze again. "Connie Ferguson told me she's big as a house."

"Did she," Lucien said flatly, running his hand through his hair. "Didn't your husband preach recently about vanity being a sin?"

Mabel tapped her fingers against her thigh and sighed. "So that's no excuse not to marry the girl. It's just that Connie made your bride sound so…so…"

"What?" he asked sharply. "Disreputable? Question-able? *Un*attractive?"

"Attraction in marriage is important, Lucien," she said, wagging her finger.

"Quite right. But who says I do not find her attractive, simply because Connie Ferguson doesn't?"

"That's true." She looked at the floor. "Forgive my prying—I was wrong to bring it up. Who you marry is entirely up to you." She absently brushed at her skirt, then looked at him. "Ten o'clock Saturday morning."

Lucien sighed and smiled. "Right. And thank you for looking out for me, Mabel."

"I just want to see you happy. I've been witness to so many wonderful weddings over the years, couples still going strong and loving each other more every day. I want you to have the same, that's all."

Lucien nodded. Mabel and Pastor James Lewis had no children, but had adopted the citizens of Nowhere as their own over the years. They were a precious couple that looked out for everyone. "Thank you," he said again.

He left the preacher's house and returned to the bank. He worked to finish up before closing time and didn't want to stay late—he wanted to take Billie to dinner again and inform her of their wedding date. He hoped she didn't feel rushed—Saturday was only four days away. In truth, he didn't want to wait that long, but if Billie needed more time he'd bear it. She was worth waiting for.

It wasn't that he wanted to rush her into his bed, though that did have strong appeal. It was because she seemed so…lost. She was a woman drifting, with no place to anchor or call her own. He wanted to give her that stability—and a lot of things he hadn't thought of before. He wanted to show her things, teach her things, give to her parts of himself he'd never given anyone else.

He knew something was wrong, but still didn't know what. It was more than the obvious, the incident that caused her injury. Could it be she felt she wasn't ready to marry? It was possible. He was a nurturer by nature, and Billie Jane Sneed needed someone to take great care with her heart, especially after what she'd been through. But he didn't want her to think he pitied her, and especially didn't want her to think he was marrying her out of pity.

Mabel wasn't the first to ask if he was having second thoughts. Mr. Davis had brought it up this morning and he hadn't met Billie either. Who knew what Nellie had told her husband? And how many more people would try to talk him out of marrying Billie before the day was out, not to mention the week? Well, he knew what he wanted, even if they didn't. He couldn't live his life on their opinions.

"Lucien, what are you doing wandering around?" Spencer Riley asked as he passed the sheriff's office.

"Good afternoon, Spencer," he said with a nod. "I'm just heading back to the bank after speaking with Mabel Lewis."

"Ah. Where's Pastor Lewis?"

"Out at the Johnson place. Old Man Johnson's sick. I don't think it's anything serious, though."

"I ought to stop by on my way home. So were you talking to Mabel about your wedding date?"

"I sure was." Lucien grinned. "Saturday morning at ten, if you'd like to attend."

Spencer shoved his hat back. "So you're going to go through with it, eh?"

Lucien groaned. "Saints preserve me, not you, too?"

"Beg pardon?"

"Never mind. Yes, I'm going to marry my lovely mail-order bride come Saturday, provided she has no objections." Anyone else with objections could, in the words of one of his Yale professors, go take a long walk off a short pier.

"If *she* has none?" Spencer said in surprise. "I'd think it'd be the other way around."

"Why would you think that?" Lucien pressed. "Based on what you saw when the stage pulled in?"

"Well, I got a good eyeful, like everyone else. You sure this is what you want?"

Lucien counted to five before answering. "Yes, it is. I sent for a bride. Miss Sneed is what I got. And I will have you know she exceeded my wildest expectations. Do you have a problem with that, *Sheriff*?"

Spencer held up his hands. "Whoa, no need to get uppity. I'm just saying…"

"Yes, you are, and now you can kindly *stop* saying. I've made up my mind and I'm getting married. Just because *you* don't think she's right for me doesn't mean *I* think she's any less a woman."

Spencer chuckled. "On the contrary, Lucien. She's more woman than I could handle."

Lucien seethed. "Beauty is in the eye of the beholder, Spencer."

Spencer looked him in the eyes. "I'm just making sure you're doing this because you want to, friend, not because you feel obligated to."

"Thank you, but be assured I want to." Lucien took a few deep breaths to cool his anger. "It seems to me people are judging Billie on her looks—or rather, their opinion of her looks—and not on what matters most or what I think of her. That woman has been through a horrible ordeal. She's scarred not just on the outside, but the inside—I'd stake my life on it. And even then, I find her…" Another breath while he searched for the right word. "…*enchanting*."

"Well," Spencer said. "Then forget I said anything. If you're sure you're getting a good woman, that's good enough for me. And everyone in town knows she's getting a good man."

Lucien unclenched the fists he didn't realize he'd made. There was no sense getting angry with Spencer—like Mabel, he was just looking out for him. However ham-handedly. "Thank you, Spencer. That means a lot."

Spencer nodded. "You're welcome. And the wife and I will be there Saturday, good Lord willing and the creek don't rise."

"See you then." Lucien turned and strode away, praying that no one else asked him if he was really going to marry Billie. If anyone did, he was liable to land himself in one of Spencer's jail cells for assault.

Chapter Ten

Billie paced in her room. Lucien would arrive any minute to take her to dinner, and she was sure he'd made some sort of arrangements for her departure. The problem was, she hadn't told him where she wanted to go. He probably bought her train and stage fare back to Denver. He wouldn't pick a place at random and send her there—the man wasn't that cruel. She hoped.

But she knew such things happened. On the journey west she'd heard tale after horrific tale of abandonment, abuse and neglect. Lucien Miller wasn't neglectful; she'd give him that. He'd provided a hotel room, food and decent company. But it was all short-lived, so why not? There was a big difference between a woman in town for a few days and one staying for the rest of his life. The moment she stepped off the stage, he'd made his decision, as she knew he would. One look at her and she'd have done the same.

But that was beside the point. She needed to tell him she wanted to go to Seattle. Would he work with her? She'd consider herself fortunate if he sent her back to Denver all-expenses-paid, and she had some money left, though not much. But what could she do? She was in no position to look a gift horse in the mouth.

If she was careful, she could find a place to stay in Denver quickly enough, and find a laborer's job if she disguised herself again. That really would be her best option. She wasn't Maitred the apprentice dress-maker—that girl had a skill. What could Billie do that she was proud of? Nothing, when one got down to it. She'd been there for her father after her mother died— that was her job, her purpose for living. She might not have had a husband, but at least she had Papa. Now that he was gone, she felt adrift.

The knock at the door made her jump. She put a hand over her racing heart and answered it. "Mr. Miller," she said in surprise.

"Please, call me Lucien," he insisted. "Are you all right?"

"Quite," she said, smiling shyly. Now where did that come from? She shook herself to regain her wits—the mere sight of the man took her breath away. "I wasn't expecting you this early, I'm afraid."

He smiled. "Well, this day has been full of surprises— at least mine has. How about yours? Did you enjoy your tea?"

"Yes, very much. The ladies were…nice."

"You hesitated," he mused. "Did Nellie Davis be- have herself?"

"Actually, she did." She stepped into the hall. "And the conversation was very uplifting. There was a lot of talk about forgiveness."

"Forgiveness?" he said, impressed. "Well, that is something. Sounds like I missed a good tea."

She nodded as her cheeks warmed. Oh, for Heaven's

sake, she needed to get a hold of herself! She was about to be sent packing, after all.

"Since it's a bit early for dinner, would you like to take a walk with me?"

"A walk?"

"Yes, so we can discuss things."

Billie looked at the floor. "Oh yes. Of course."

"And I thought you might need a few items from the mercantile."

Her head came up. "No. I already purchased what I needed, but thank you."

"Oh," he said, looking disappointed. "Everything? You're sure?"

She nodded. At least he was trying to be accommodating. "But thank you for thinking of me."

"Of course I'm thinking of you. Why wouldn't I?"

She didn't know what to say to that. He was being very nice and trying to do what he could, and for that she was grateful. Finally, she settled on, "You're most kind."

He stepped closer. "Let me know if you need anything, won't you?"

"Of course." She stepped away, went into the room and snatched her reticule. "Shall we?"

He was suddenly behind her, a hand on her shoulder. "Billie, I want to be your friend."

She turned and looked into his eyes. *Friend.* Well, of course—he didn't want to part on bad terms. If she were in his position, she would want the same. It was either that or he felt incredibly guilty. "Lucien, it's not as if we're going to be writing to each other anymore."

"Of course not, but I think it's good to be friends, don't you?"

Her heart sank. Definitely guilt. "You don't have to try so hard, you know."

"Try? Of course I'm going to try, Billie." He shrugged. "Besides, I can't help myself. Naturally I want to get to know you better."

She stared at him in confusion. "You are a different sort, Mr. Miller."

"*Lucien*. Now come with me—there's something I want to show you." He offered her his arm.

She took it—it would be rude not to—and they went downstairs, past the front desk (complete with a gawking Mrs. Ferguson) and out the hotel door. She wasn't sure what to do. He was acting as if everything was fine, that he wasn't about to ship her off as a reject. This was all so bizarre.

"Billie, what's wrong?" he asked.

"If you don't know, Mr. Miller, then I don't know what to tell you." She was done being gentle about this. In fact, she was getting angry. How dare he assume that, kind as he was, stringing her along like this was okay? And she was letting him get away with it. Well, time to put a stop to that.

"I'm not clairvoyant, Billie. If there's something wrong, you have to tell me."

She pulled away, clasped her hands behind her back and looked him in the eyes. "You wanted to discuss details?"

He sighed. "Yes, I did." He motioned to the boardwalk and took a step forward. She walked beside him but not arm in arm—it just didn't feel right. He had to understand that.

When he didn't say anything for a minute, she broke the silence. "Details?"

"Saturday morning at ten o'clock," he stated. "Will that suit?"

"Yes, but I'm surprised you didn't arrange for something sooner."

"It's the soonest I could manage. If you're unwilling to wait, though…"

"Saturday it is, then." She tried to keep her voice from shaking. Four days. She would have to endure this for *four more days*. Could she do it?

"Do you require anything?" he asked. "Anything special you'd like to wear?"

She gave him a sidelong glance, then quickly looked away. "One of my dresses will suit."

"If that's what you wish. I just thought…"

Billie stopped. "You thought what, that I would want to dress in something special for the occasion?"

He looked thoroughly confused. "Most women do."

"Oh, do they? So I'm not the first?"

"Of course not—you've met some of the others. And I'm sure you won't be the last."

Billie gasped. "Mr. Miller, how could you?" It was getting harder and harder to keep the tears at bay. So she wasn't the first rejected bride, was she? And some of them had been stuck here, unable to leave? Which ones, she wondered. And what was this place, a town full of heartbreakers?

"I certainly didn't mean to offend. And honestly, I'm not sure how I have. If you'd be so kind as to enlighten me…"

"Mr. Miller, I don't think you need to be enlightened. Saturday at ten—have it your way. Now if you will excuse me, I have a headache and want to go back to my room." She spun on her heel and headed for the hotel.

"Billie, wait!"

She kept going. If she turned around, she might slap him. This wasn't kindness, it was a mockery!

He caught up and put a hand on her shoulder. "Billie…"

She spun away and glared at him, fists clenched at her sides. "Mr. Miller!"

"Billie! Tell me what has you so upset."

She spun to face him, her mouth open in shock. "Surely you jest."

"I do, but I'm not jesting right now."

Billie rolled her eyes. "Saturday at ten. Thank you for the information, and thank you for all you've done. But I really must go now." She turned and marched away, having had enough of Lucien Miller, Nowhere, her promise to her father and anything except going back to her room and sobbing in fury into a pillow.

Lucien stood in shock, staring at Billie's retreating form. Should he go after her? "No, no," he said to himself. He wasn't sure why she was so upset, but he knew he'd better let her calm down before speaking with her again.

Still, he wondered. Had something happened during her tea? He rubbed his chin and turned around. Perhaps he should pay a visit to the mercantile and find out— Charlotte could tell him if anything was amiss. Perhaps Nellie had said something…something that needed to be forgiven. Is that why Billie brought up forgiveness? Drat that Nellie Davis! She'd been a thorn in Nowhere's side for years.

It was bad enough he had to work with Mr. Davis at the bank, listening to him lament his wife. But Mr.

Davis was a decent sort, despite his terrible taste in wives. According to him, she'd always been uppity—a Southern belle born to money and privilege, who lost it all in the war. Apparently, someone forgot to tell Nellie that there were no more slaves at her beck and call and she couldn't just treat people however she wanted.

Thank Heaven Mr. Davis had come west when he did. That alone had tempered her, according to him. He told Lucien once that on the trip west, he'd recognized some of his own shortcomings and vowed never to be that person again. Lucien admired him for that. He'd become a better man and wanted to stay that way. Alas, Nellie was still far behind him.

Lucien stepped into the mercantile and went straight to the counter. "Good afternoon, Mrs. Quinn," he greeted.

Betsy looked up from the ledger she'd been writing in. "Lucien, what brings you in today? Do you have a list?"

"No, but I'd like to talk with Charlotte if I may."

Betsy smiled. "Is this regarding your wedding?"

"Peripherally, yes."

She clapped her hands and hurried around the counter. "I'll go fetch her!"

Lucien shook his head as she hurried down the hall. He'd let Charlotte tell her mother-in-law this had nothing to do with wedding preparations. Right now he didn't have the stomach for it.

"Why, Lucien Miller, what can I do for you?" Charlotte said as she entered the storefront, Betsy on her heels.

From the looks of it, her mother-in-law was about to find out anyway. *Oh well*, he thought. "I was wondering, did anything…untoward happen between Miss Sneed and your mother at tea this afternoon?"

Betsy and Charlotte exchanged a quick look. "Certainly not," Betsy said. "We had a fine time, didn't we, Charlotte?"

"Yes, we did. In fact, my mother was most civil."

"She was?" Lucien immediately regretted the surprise in his voice, but could he honestly be blamed?

"I know it's hard to believe, but it's true. After all these years I think my mother is finally starting to change."

"And it's a wonderful thing too," Betsy added.

Lucien rubbed his chin. "This makes no sense. Miss Sneed seemed upset over something, but I can't figure out what. All I did was tell her the time I'd arranged for the wedding and ask if she wanted to wear anything special."

"Does she?" Betsy asked, hopeful.

"Mother Quinn…" Charlotte pleaded.

"Oh, you know this has me on pins and needles. I can only imagine what Leona's going through."

"Leona is busy at home with her grandchildren," Charlotte said.

"Hmph," Betsy replied. "At least one of us is." She went behind the counter.

Charlotte ignored the dig. "I don't know what to tell you, Lucien. We had a lovely time. And Abbey and I both offered to help with a dress if Billie wanted."

Lucien smiled at the sound of his bride's name. "I'd like to see her in a fine dress. But if that's not what she wants, I won't force her. Maybe she thought I was…"

Charlotte shrugged helplessly. "I couldn't say. But

we did talk about it, and she said she'd let us know. She must have decided against it."

"Yes, you're probably right. Well then, I suppose there's nothing else for me to do but to work out a misunderstanding with my bride."

"Let us know if you need any help," Betsy called from somewhere in the back.

"Don't worry, Mrs. Quinn, I will." He smiled in amusement, winked at Charlotte and left. At least neither one of *them* had tried to talk him out of marrying Billie. He'd had his fill of that. But now what? He didn't want anything to come between them. After all, what she wore at their wedding was a minor detail. And if Saturday was too soon, well, he'd postpone…

Lucien stopped when he reached the bottom of the mercantile steps and smacked his forehead. "Of course, why didn't I think of that?" He turned, went back up and inside again. "Charlotte, Mrs. Quinn!"

Both were behind the counter now. "Forget something, Lucien?" Charlotte asked.

"I arranged for our wedding to take place on Saturday. Miss Sneed got upset after I gave her the date. Perhaps she wants a wedding dress and didn't know how to tell me, and now she's worried there won't be time to make one."

"Could be," Charlotte conceded.

Mrs. Quinn beamed and raised her hands in the air. "Praise the Lord, I'm back in business!"

Lucien and Charlotte laughed nervously. "Does this mean you're going to let Leona know?" Charlotte asked.

"Heavens, no—I'm keeping this to myself for a few days. Now let me see… I'm thinking the white would look best on Billie. What do you think, Charlotte?"

Charlotte laughed. "I think someone needs to warn Billie. You're liable to scare her so bad, she'll take the first stage back to Denver."

Betsy slapped the feather duster in her hand on the counter. "Enough out of you. Now let's get to work—Billie needs our help!"

Lucien chuckled at the proprietress. In spite of Nowhere's little quirks, its people were endearing. He just hoped that Billie would think so too.

Chapter Eleven

Billie wiped a tear from her eye. She was tougher than this, blast it! Why was Lucien's refusal to marry her bothering her so? No…not so much his refusal as the way he was handling it, drawing it out, being so *friendly*. The hotel room, her meals, arranging stage and train fare elsewhere—didn't he realize it would make the final rejection that much more painful? Not to mention make her feel so…so…

"…Unworthy." She whispered the word, but might as well have had it tattooed on her forehead. She deserved the rejection—what man wanted a disfigured woman who was taller and brawnier than most men? Devil take it, she probably weighed as much as Lucien did. She could live with that, and had. But the kindness and generosity was just confusing.

She shrugged the thoughts off, opened her trunk and pulled out her pink day dress. Saturday was four days away and she'd been wearing her purple traveling clothes for days already—they could probably stand up by themselves. She'd have to see about getting them laundered. But where? This wasn't the type of hotel where one could drop off laundry and have it done. She'd either have to do it herself in the nearest bathtub or find someone else to do it.

"I'll ask Charlotte," she said to herself. She was a native—she'd know who took in laundry around there. She changed her clothes, touched up her hair and left for the mercantile, hoping they were still open—it was almost dinnertime.

Thankfully, it was, and she went up the front steps and inside. "Charlotte?"

Mrs. Quinn looked up and smiled widely. "Billie, how nice to see you again!"

Billie forced a smile as she went to the counter. "Hello, Mrs. Quinn."

"Call me Betsy. Now how can I help?"

"Well, I need my traveling clothes laundered and I was wondering…"

"Oh my heavens, is that all? Can't it wait until you're settled?"

Billie blinked a few times. Was the woman serious? Did she really think…oh, never mind. "I'd rather get it done sooner."

"But child, this is a busy week for you—let it go until later." She looked Billie over with approval. "My, that's a pretty frock. And the matching eyepatch is darling!"

Billie grimaced. She'd put on the pink patch with the white lace frill she hated so much—well, at least someone liked it. "Thank you." She'd ask someone else about finding a laundress—obviously Mrs. Quinn wasn't going to help her on that, and she didn't want to press it.

The bell over the door rang. "Billie, there you are," Lucien said with relief. "Working things out?"

"We were getting to that, Lucien," Betsy said. "But I suppose you'd like to take this young lady to dinner?"

"Yes, and I'm sure you'll be wanting yours."

A chill went up Billie's spine. She wasn't sure she could stand being around Lucien Miller much longer. If he tortured her any more than he already had, she might hit him.

Betsy nodded. "Charlotte's cooking tonight, thank Heaven. Ever since she married my Matthew, my life has been so much easier. I just wish…well, never mind. You two have a lovely evening."

"We will." Lucien took Billie's arm. His hand was larger than she thought and incredibly warm. She shivered again, but without the dread that accompanied the last one. This one was more like anticipation—but of what?

Betsy came around the counter. "I'll lock up after you go."

"Good night," Lucien replied and led Billie out. She looked at their locked limbs as her heart raced. What was he doing? Oh, probably just keeping up appearances—Betsy Quinn didn't know she was leaving. Or did she?

She puzzled over it as Lucien led her down to the boardwalk. "I thought we'd have dinner, then take a walk," he said.

"Saturday," she mumbled.

"Oh, is that what you and Mrs. Quinn were discussing?"

"Er, yes and no. Does she know?"

"About Saturday? Of course she does. She even volunteered to help with anything you might need."

Billie's gut twisted and she stopped. "She…did?"

"Yes, as did Charlotte. Do you want their help?"

Aghast, her hand flew to her mouth. "How could you?"

"What's this?" he said, worried. "Billie, what's wrong?"

"What's wrong?!" she yelped. "This whole thing has been wrong from the start! I should have arranged for my own way out of here! You didn't even wait to… to…" It was too much. Her emotions, no matter how hard she'd tried to suppress them since her father's murder, came bubbling to the surface. "You scalawag!" She wrenched her arm from his and ran.

"Billie!" She heard his rapid footfalls behind her and ran faster. What a fool she was! Why had she put herself through such humiliation? Yes, her promise to Father, but still, what was she thinking?

Lucien grabbed her arm and brought them both to a stumbling stop. "Billie, what do you think you're doing?"

"Let go of me," she snarled, and tried to yank her arm away.

"No. I will not let go, not until you tell me what's been going on. Don't you *want* to get married?"

"What…?" Then the last six words registered in Billie's brain and stunned her into silence. She wanted to laugh at him, and might have if her knees hadn't given out.

"Billie!" Lucien cried, and did something she didn't expect. He caught her! No man had ever managed that before, or even tried. He eased her to the edge of the boardwalk, sat her down there and settled beside her, his arm around her shoulder. "Are you all right?"

She stared at him, dumbfounded. "I should ask that of you."

He blinked and stuttered, "Of c-course I'm all right, you silly woman. I'm not the one who almost fainted."

She studied the concerned look on his face. Was she all right? Because she certainly didn't understand what was going on. "I'm fine. Please, just leave me be."

His face fell. "Then...you don't want to get married."

She stopped breathing. Did she hear him right? "What?"

"I asked if you still wanted to get married." He removed his arm and took her hand between his. "Because I do. I hope I haven't done something to make you think otherwise."

Billie gasped. Good Lord above, had she made a mistake? If so, this went way beyond a little misunderstanding—she'd been misinterpreting *everything*. She looked at the near-empty street, trying to think through it all. "Well, blow me down..."

"I beg your pardon?"

"I..." She swallowed hard. "I think that maybe I've not been..."

"What, darling?"

Her jaw dropped at the endearment, and she looked at him in surprise while trying to work up her courage. "I don't—no. I can't believe that..."

"Believe what?" He shook his head. "I'm afraid I don't understand."

She took a deep breath and let her words tumble out. "I thought you wanted me to go. I mean, you bought me stage and train fare for Saturday. It made perfect sense—I mean, how could you even think of marrying *me*? Of course you were going to give me the push and try someone else. You're so kind and generous and very handsome—oh dear, I suppose I shouldn't have said that, but there it is—and there's no reason you should have to settle for some disfigured giantess, so naturally I—"

"Wait!" He let go of her hand and sat back, staring at her as if she'd just appeared out of thin air. "You think I don't want to marry you?!"

"I mean, you've been very kind, Mr. Miller, but I understand…"

He ran a hand through his hair, then took her by the shoulders and turned her toward him. "Whatever gave you that idea?"

Billie blinked. "What else could it be?"

He stared dumbfounded at her for a second or two. "It could be this." And he pulled her close and kissed her.

Billie squirmed in his arms, but he held her fast—not harshly, but firmly enough that she wasn't going anywhere. Egads, he was strong! And his kiss was not only warm and gentle, but it felt as if he had just given her a message—something along the lines of "there is no turning back from this moment." Could it really be… it seemed too much to ask for, too unlikely to occur, but…was it possible?

Lucien broke the kiss, sat back and stared at her, still holding her shoulders. "Does that convince you?" When she didn't speak, he added, "I want to marry you. Specifically, this Saturday at ten o'clock. Who told you I was talking about anything else?"

"I…well…"

"Well, what? How could you think…ohhhh." He looked up the street, fire in his eyes. "Did Nellie Davis have anything to do with this?"

She shook her head, still dumbfounded by his kiss and his declaration.

"Mrs. Ferguson?"

She shook her head again, and finally her voice worked. "No. No one told me that…except me…" And to her—and Lucien's—further shock, she burst into tears.

Lucien said nothing, just pulled her close, resting her head on his muscular shoulder.

And as the tears drained out, she suddenly saw everything so clearly: her guilt over her father's dying wish, her confidence that no one would want her, the years of being passed over by every man worth his salt she'd ever met…and Lucien's words. "I want to marry you." He did? Really? Why? No—never mind why. He did—that should be enough…

"Billie…" Lucien wrapped his arms around her and patted her back. "Look, I don't know why you thought what you did, but it doesn't matter. I do want to marry you. It's why I sent for a mail-order bride."

She pulled away, confusion on her face. "But you got me."

"Yes, I did. And I am so glad. You're beyond what I'd ever hoped for."

She stared at him, completely flummoxed.

"Billie." He looked her in the eye. "Do you want to marry me?"

"But…you could have most anyone…"

"Mrs. Pettigrew sent me someone far better than 'most anyone'."

She gasped so hard she almost choked. No one had ever truly wanted her, not even *before* she was scarred and half-blinded. Was the man daft? Did he not see her? "Me?" she whispered.

"Oh yes, you. The moment you got off the stage, I was ruined for anyone else."

"My." She hung her head, unable to grasp it. He really wanted...her. Big, wide, ungainly, half-sighted, slashed-up her. "Are you insane?"

Lucien gently released her and chuckled. "Not that I last noticed."

"Because how could you...what... I... I mean, look at me!" She spread her arms.

"Gladly, my dear. For as long as we both shall live."

"Mr. Miller..."

He sighed. "*Lucien.*"

"Very well—Lucien." She straightened and folded her hands in her lap. "You don't have to lie to me or flatter me. I have seen mirrors—I know how I look. I'm not stupid."

He frowned. "No, but it's becoming clear you're a bit thick-headed."

"What?!"

"Billie, I imagine you've been told how others see you. You've told me how you see yourself. But I don't see that. I see a woman who meets every criterion for beauty I have, save for the missing eye, and I'm willing to live with that as a minor imperfection that assures me I'm not marrying an *actual* goddess. I hold no responsibility for what anyone else thinks, but that's not flattery, that's my view. Take it or leave it." He blinked, as if he'd just shocked himself with his words.

But not as much as he'd shocked *her.* She closed her eyes, trying to believe what he'd just said. "G-goddess?"

"If you were living in ancient Rome or Greece, they would have built temples to you."

Improve upon *that*! "You're not marrying me just because you feel you have to?"

"Not in the slightest—I want to. Now, unless you give me a good reason why we shouldn't, Billie Jane Sneed, we are getting married Saturday and that's that."

Billie looked at him. The man had to be out of his head if he wanted to marry her. But she had no better offers… "I do have one reason."

"You do?"

Billie nodded. "I… I want a proper dress."

He paused in thought. "Er…a wedding dress?"

"Yes. Mrs. Quinn offered to help me with one."

"Betsy Quinn?" he said, his voice cracking. "Oh dear. Do you have any idea what she'll do to you? Let alone Mrs. Riley once she catches wind of this?"

"I've been warned, but I still want help. I understand they've helped almost every bride in this town."

"Well, a lucky few have escaped their clutches…but if that's what you want, I won't stand in your way. They may do their worst." He stood and offered his hand. "If you feel up for it, shall we go to dinner?"

"All right." She let him help her up—the first time a man had done that with her, or been able to—and put her arm through his. For a glorious moment, she felt as if he was afraid to let her go. But it passed. She was just Billie, after all, the woman no man wanted. Until now, if Lucien was in fact sane. Maybe she should ask around about that. If he wasn't, she couldn't let him go through with it, her promise to Father or no.

She scanned their surroundings—had anyone seen their kiss? It didn't seem so—no gasps of surprise or

disgust had drawn her notice. The meaning of the kiss...
well, he'd said what he thought it was. But could she believe it? It all seemed so far-fetched that he would want
her, but either he was a liar, a lunatic or...completely
sincere in his affections.

They entered Hank's and sat at the same table as before. Hank himself took their orders and went to fetch
their drinks. "Nellie isn't working tonight?" she asked.

"You just had tea with her this afternoon," Lucien
pointed out.

Billie blushed. "Oh yes, I forgot."

He sat back in his chair and watched her a moment.
"You're still upset, I can tell."

She shrugged, looking down at the table. "Perhaps
a little."

He leaned toward her. "Billie, if we're to be married,
we have to trust each other."

Her chest tightened, making it hard to breathe. Why
did he have to be so *nice*? She wanted to trust him, but
did she dare? He'd be no different than all the rest of
the men she knew. She wasn't pretty or dainty—closer
to the proverbial bull in a china shop than a china doll.
Yet the look he was giving her said he was not only serious, but smitten. How could that be?

"Billie." He reached a hand across the table, palm
up in invitation. "You can trust me."

Her throat became thick, and she felt tears at the back
of her eyes. What was happening?

"Sweetheart, please."

A squeak of despair escaped her. She wanted this
man. But did he really want her? He might think he did,
because he'd convinced himself he was doing the right

thing. Any other man would have seen her getting off that stage and left her high and dry.

But it was obvious Lucien Miller wasn't just any man. Hope rose in her heart, and this time she was too frazzled to shove it back down.

"Billie," he said softly.

She swallowed the lump in her throat. "Lucien…"

"And I'm Hank—here's your iced teas." The proprietor set the glasses on the table, turned and went back to the kitchen.

"Good timing, Hank," Lucien grumbled under his breath. He sighed and put his other hand out to her. "Trust me?"

She looked at his open hands, and slowly, put hers in them. "I… I'll try."

Lucien smiled gently. "That's all I could ask for."

Billie forced a smile back. Could it really be? Well, she was still going to ask around about his potential insanity. Trust would take time.

Chapter Twelve

What happened to her? That's what Lucien wanted
to know. Billie was terrified, and the thought made
his blood boil. If he ever got his hands on the man that
harmed her, he'd…he'd…well, haul him before the law
and make sure he got his due punishment. He knew
he couldn't bring himself to kill a man. Maim, maybe.

But more importantly, he had to convince Billie he
wouldn't hurt her. She must be wary after what she'd been
through and he needed to remember that. "Shall we pray?"

Her eyes went to her hands in his, and she slowly
nodded.

He gave both a squeeze, smiled and bowed his head.
"Lord, we thank You for this bountiful blessing and
this day. Amen." He raised his head and smiled gently.
"Maybe if we're lucky, there's cherry pie for dessert."
He gave her hands another squeeze and released them.
She pulled them across the table and put them in her
lap instead of on her sandwich.

She reminded him of a filly his father had owned—
a beautiful, wild creature that had been abused by its
former master. His father bought it to save it, and spent

many an evening with the animal in the family stables, earning the poor thing's trust. It took lots of time, but eventually the little filly grew to be a fine mare that would do anything for his father. How long, he wondered, would it take Billie?

Lucien watched her reach for the sandwich, pick it up and take a tiny bite. For all her size, she was incredibly feminine, like an Amazon caught unawares. Off the battlefield with her guard down and no one looking, she could be a woman and not a warrior.

He took a sip of his iced tea, then picked up his sandwich. "You'll thank me later."

She cocked her head at him as she chewed.

"Ordering the sandwich, I mean," he explained. "If you ever try the stew, you'll understand why."

She almost smiled as she swallowed. "I'll try not to forget."

They continued to eat, chatting about things of little interest between bites. He didn't want to upset her and wasn't sure what to talk about, so he let her pick the subjects. But she wasn't choosing any that led to what really needed to be discussed: the wedding.

Well, he had to do something… "I do want to show you the house tomorrow. I'll ask Charlotte if she can accompany us."

"Your house?" Billie wiped her mouth with her napkin.

"Our house. You're going to live there, so I want you to look at it, see if you'd like to make any changes…"

"But…"

Be gentle, he thought to himself. *Don't scare her.* "I'll admit it probably needs a few feminine touches. I tend to like cream and brown, but you might prefer pastels. And I didn't do much with the curtains."

"Oh," she said with a sigh. "I see."

"Do you?"

"Oh yes," she said, a little too quickly.

If she was agreeing just to appease him, she still wasn't open to trusting him. Did she honestly think she was just biding her time until he sent her back to Denver? Wasn't she going to be surprised when that didn't happen! "Charlotte has the most wonderful catalogue at the mercantile. I ordered some new china for you." He waited for her reaction.

"But…you couldn't have." She set her sandwich down. "You don't know me. How could you have known what I like?"

He smiled as his shoulders shook with silent mirth. "Well, I ordered them for my mail-order bride, which is you. Charlotte assured me that any woman would love the set, and you're a woman. Thus, they were ordered for you. *Quod erat demonstrandum*."

She pretended to wipe her mouth, but he could tell she was covering up a smile. But was it a smile of amusement or of nerves? Every time he made an attempt to convince her of his commitment to their future union, she seemed to cringe in fear, as if she was already convinced it was never going to happen…

…*Great Scott, that was it!* That's exactly what she thought. He stiffened. She'd suffered a horrible ordeal. Many people would consider her damaged goods. A few had over the last couple of days—otherwise, why would they question his desire to marry her? But he *would* marry her. Billie Jane Sneed was a woman meant to be loved, not discarded. "I'll show you the china tomorrow when we see the house," he said with a smile. "And the garden as well."

Her smile now was clearly forced. But she didn't say no. Progress? He suppressed a sigh. This wasn't going to be easy. Billie was frightened, abused, hurt and so used to disappointment that she probably didn't expect life to hand her anything else. He'd have to do something about that, and that would just have to take time. And he was willing to spend a lifetime on it. "Pie?"

This smile was genuine. "Sounds fine."

Lucien waved Hank over. "What kind of pies today, Hank?"

"Apple and cherry. You want coffee with those?"

"Please, and two pieces of the cherry."

"Coming right up," Hank said. "Baked them myself."

"Wonderful," Lucien said as the proprietor walked away.

"Wonderful?" Billie echoed.

"Hank doesn't bake everything around here. Some of the local women bake pies, and he purchases them to sell to his customers. But he's better at it than most of them—he just doesn't always have the time."

"I had no idea." She fiddled with her napkin. "I'm not a very good baker. I'm not a very good anything."

Lucien stared at her. He was sure she wasn't the type of woman to feel sorry for herself. *Ergo*, she was stating fact, or at least her perception. He could handle that. "Whatever skills you think you lack, you can learn. I wasn't good at gardening when I was younger, but I don't do so bad now."

She smiled. "I've never had a garden. I was too often away at sea with my father."

He rested his arms on the table, a smile on his face. "I bet you and your father had some grand adventures."

Her face lit up. "Oh yes, we did."

"Tell me about one," he coaxed.

She smiled again. "My goodness, I wouldn't know where to start."

"How about the last voyage you took together—where did you go?"

"Well, we sailed from Liverpool to Santander in northern Spain, with a cargo of textiles and other manufactured goods. Then back again with a hull full of wool for the textile mills. We did that tour several times."

"What would you and your father do when you reached a destination?" he asked, genuinely curious.

"After seeing to the unloading of cargo, we'd have dinner somewhere, maybe see some things of interest if there was time. But Father's primary concern was with getting the return cargo loaded, not sightseeing. That last trip, once we returned to Liverpool, Father sold the *Nina Jane* and booked our passage to America."

Lucien noted the sadness in her eyes. "I wish I'd known him."

She met his gaze for a moment, then closed her eye. "I think he would have liked you."

"As his future son-in-law, I would hope so," he said with a grin. She bowed her head and he wondered what she was thinking. "I imagine you miss the sea."

"Yes. But I miss Father more."

Lucien fought the urge to get up, walk around the table and take her in his arms. Not because it would be highly improper, but because he didn't want to spook her. He wanted to comfort her, but she might feel more trapped than comforted. He needed to be careful.

"Here we are." Hank set a tray on the table and unloaded two cups of coffee and two plates of cherry pie. He looked at Billie. "Do you bake? I could always use another woman's baking in this place. You getting hitched to Lucien here works good for me, since his place is just at the edge of town."

Lucien saw Billie pale and stepped in. "I'm afraid my bride and I will be too busy at first, Hank. She'll have to bestow her baking talents upon you at a later time... Christmas, maybe?"

Hank frowned. "I was thinking more along the lines of in a week or two. Or at least for the town picnic."

Lucien smiled reassuringly. "I'm afraid not...wait. What's this about a town picnic?"

"There's talk about having a big to-do at Old Man Johnson's place," Hank said. "Don't tell me no one's told you folks at the bank yet?"

"No one's said a word. Besides, Mabel Lewis told me earlier this week her husband was visiting Mr. Johnson, because he wasn't feeling well."

"I heard he was feeling poorly too, but it seems it's his idea."

Lucien glanced between Hank and Billie. "Perhaps he wants it there because he's worried he won't be with us much longer."

Billie gasped. "What?"

"He *is* old," Hank pointed out. "Why do you think we call him Old Man Johnson?"

She shrugged. "How could I know?"

"It's fine, darling," Lucien said. "Nothing for you to worry about." He turned back to Hank. "I'll stop by the sheriff's office today and ask Spencer—I recall him saying he'd check in on him, so he should know."

"Good idea," Hank agreed, then glanced at Billie. "Sheriff Riley lives next door to the Johnsons."

"Come to think of it, I've not seen Bernice or Warren in town," Lucien recalled, then explained it to Billie. "Warren is Mr. Johnson's grandson, and Bernice is Warren's wife. She came to Nowhere as a mail-order bride just like you. I think you'd like her. In fact... I should take you out to the Johnson farm this week and introduce you to Warren and Bernice. I could check on Old Man Johnson while we're at it—maybe we can help with something."

"With what?" Billie asked.

"I don't know, but I'm sure we'll find out. Up for a little drive tomorrow?" Maybe if she felt useful in some capacity, she'd be less fearful. Besides, Bernice was a sweetheart, and he'd heard she felt completely out of place when she first came to Nowhere.

She nodded. "But don't you have to work?"

"Yes, but it's not going to hurt the bank if I leave a bit early. I know Mr. Davis won't mind."

"Find out what you can about this picnic too," Hank asked. "If there's going to be one, I'll have to figure out if I need to close up for the day."

"We'll report back everything we know," Lucien assured him.

Hank look surprised for a moment, smiled and retreated to the kitchen.

Lucien winked at Billie, picked up his fork and began to eat his pie. Hopefully this would be another step in his bride-to-be's healing.

The next day Lucien showed up at the hotel with a horse and buggy. "He's beautiful," Billie commented as she stroked the horse's soft muzzle. "Is he yours?"

"She—her name is Marybelle—and no, sadly, she is not mine, I rented her from the livery."

"You don't own a horse?"

"I've never had a need to. If I want to go somewhere I rent one—more cost-effective." He helped her climb onto the buggy seat, walked around to the other side and climbed up himself. "Do you drive?"

"No, never in my life." She looked around. "What will people think of the two of us driving to the Johnson farm alone?"

"You're my bride-to-be," he said gently, "and we'll be married in a few days. I don't think anyone will pay us any mind."

She smiled gently. "Still, perhaps Charlotte could come."

"I asked, but she's busy this afternoon at the mercantile and can't make it. Don't worry, it's less than two miles to the Johnson farm—nowhere near enough time to ravish you, my dear. And if I tried, you'd no doubt give me the thrashing of my life, so…" That made her smile, and he smiled back.

"Charlotte told me that the Rileys and Johnsons have been in this area for a long time," Billie mentioned.

Lucien nodded, appreciating her willingness to have a conversation. "I'm told they were among the original settlers here—good families, both. Did you know Clayton Riley was sheriff before his brother Spencer?"

"No, I didn't."

"Clayton quit the law to take care of their orchards full time. He'd lost his first wife while working the farm, which soured him on agriculture, so he became sheriff to distance himself. Then his family sent away for his current wife Summer—without his knowledge." He watched her eyebrows go up. "They were married

despite a series of difficulties, including that little surprise, and have been happy together ever since."

"You make it sound like a fairytale."

"For Summer I imagine it was. She came from an
orphanage in New Orleans. When she turned eighteen,
it was either become a mail-order bride or take her
chances in the streets."

She looked at him, her head cocked to one side. "Lucien Miller, are you gossiping?"

"No, this is all public knowledge—I'm just giving
you the history." He suppressed a smile. "Then Leona
Riley sent away for a bride for Spencer, and it turned
out Elle was Summer's best friend from the same orphanage."

"My, that is interesting," she said with a giggle.

Lucien was glad their conversation was lightening
her mood. She was still skittish, he could tell, but this
seemed to help. "You'll like Bernice."

"You said that last night."

"Did I? Oh yes, yes…" he teased. She laughed, and
they gazed at each other for a moment or two before he
realized they hadn't left. "I think we'd best be going,"
he said softly, trying to keep his eyes off her lips.

"Yes, we should," she agreed as her own eye skipped
between his gaze and his mouth.

Lucien shook himself, straightened and gave the
horses a slap with the lines. He didn't dare kiss her in
front of the hotel, not with Mrs. Ferguson undoubtedly
looking on, the old busybody. Stealing a kiss wouldn't
be much as scandals went, but he didn't want to rush
Billie. The poor woman had been through enough the
last few months. No wonder she was shocked at his acceptance.

Once out of town she began to relax as she saw the countryside. "It's beautiful," she said, her eye bright.

Lucien smiled. It was the first time he'd seen her with that look, and he wanted to see more of it. "Yes, especially at this time of year with the blossoms. Wait until you see it in the fall—the air is so sweet you don't want to be anywhere else. And I grew up with those legendary New England autumns, so that's saying something."

She continued to look around. "How large is the Johnson farm?"

"I'm not sure, but they do hire a few hands at harvest time. Same with the Riley spread, which is even larger. Me, I'm happy with my vegetable garden. I can't wait to show it to you."

"I look forward to seeing it."

Lucien looked at her. "You do?"

She smiled shyly and nodded.

Perhaps he was breaking through at last. He wanted her comfortable with him, wanted her trust, her heart. But it would take time well beyond their wedding day. "Do you like flowers? I have flowerbeds in front of the house, but nothing much in them yet. I look forward to seeing what you'd like me to do with them."

That got her attention. "Roses are my favorite. I don't know if I have a 'green thumb,' however."

"We can find out. And I didn't at first, but it developed in time. We can plant whatever you like—the beds are yours. Also, we have an apple tree in the backyard…"

"You do… I mean, we do?"

Lucien smiled as his chest swelled. "Yes, sweetheart. We do." He fought the urge to kiss her, but felt part of her protective wall crack, giving him a chance to step in. If he could break through and let her know he would protect her heart, love it, cherish it, maybe she would learn to protect and cherish it too.

Chapter Thirteen

❧

"...And this is my wife Bernice," Warren Johnson announced as his wife entered the parlor.

Billie studied the woman a moment. She was very thin, with light brown hair and brown eyes. "How do you do?"

"Very well, thank you. I'm so glad you could visit us today."

"I hope it's not an inconvenience," Lucien said. "But I heard your grandfather wasn't doing well and wanted to check on him."

"He's upstairs resting," Warren said. "Bernice, some tea?"

"I already put the kettle on—and just took a batch of cookies out of the oven."

"Splendid timing, then." Lucien winked at Billie.

She felt her cheeks grow hot and continued to study Bernice, who was doing the same with her. "Did you make your dress?" Bernice asked.

"No, a dressmaker did. Including the matching eye-patch." She'd donned a sky-blue day dress with navy pinstripes, and a hat and patch to match. Lucien had told her how beautiful she looked as soon as she opened her door, and again when he brought her downstairs. Mrs. Ferguson had watched them like a hawk, looking Billie up and down as if she'd just seen her for the first time.

Lucien's compliments had made her blush despite Mrs. Ferguson's scrutiny. For a moment she'd thought it was just flattery, but one thing she was learning about Lucien Miller was that he was an honest man. What she couldn't figure out was why he'd think *she* was beautiful. Maybe it was just the outfit…but then there was all that talk about ancient goddesses.

Bernice motioned Billie to join her on a loveseat. "I hear you're a mail-order bride."

"Indeed. Lucien tells me you were too."

"I was. Warren's grandfather sent for me."

"Really?" Billie looked at Warren.

Warren nodded. "There was a lot of…*surprise* bride-ordering back then. Where they forgot to tell the grooms."

"Yes," agreed Lucien. "I told Billie about the Rileys already. And Mrs. Quinn ordered one for Matthew, but she ended up marrying Tom Turner because Matthew was already in love with Charlotte—that was a comedy of errors." He rolled his eyes.

"And my grandfather did the same." Warren jabbed his chest with his thumb. "Worked out despite the bumpy beginning."

"Blimey," Billie said. "I'll have to ask Charlotte about that. And I met a few of the Weavers when I first arrived." She looked at Lucien. "Did their mother order her sons mail-order brides?"

Lucien laughed. "Oh no—you couldn't do that with

the Weaver boys. They'd never stand for it, not even from their mother. They sent for their own."

Billie closed her eyes and shook her head. "I'll never keep this straight."

"I don't even try," Bernice admitted.

Billie giggled. She was having fun with Lucien—the pleasant conversation on the drive out, enjoying each other's company in the warm afternoon sun, and now sharing tea and tales with the Johnsons.

"You'll stay for supper, won't you?" Bernice asked.

Billie glanced between Bernice and Lucien. It wasn't up to her—she hadn't rented the horse and buggy.

"Would you like to stay?" Lucien asked.

She smiled. "Yes, if that's what you wish."

He smiled back with a little shake of his head. "I asked what *you* wanted. Would you like to stay?"

Her chest warmed. He was putting her first. "Yes, I would."

"Bernice, we will be staying for supper," Lucien announced. "Now tell me about the old man—how is he, really?"

Bernice and Warren exchanged a quick look. "Not getting any younger," Warren said. "The doc says he's just slowing down from age. He can't do what he thinks he can do."

"Like climbing a tree," Bernice added. "Or moving crates of apples."

"His balance is off," Warren added. "So climbing a ladder isn't much better."

"I'm sorry to hear that," Lucien said. "Billie and I would be happy to lend a hand come harvest time."

Billie glanced at him, then at Bernice and Warren. If she agreed, she'd be planting her feet more firmly in

Nowhere. Her heart beat hard at the thought. "Oh yes," she said at last. "Whatever you need."

"Thank you, that's so kind," Bernice said. "Come harvest, we should have enough people to help."

"The hard part is keeping Grandpa off the ladders," Warren said. "His biggest fear is feeling useless. We'll have to find something else for him to do."

Billie stared at the floor. "My father was afraid of that as well."

"Was he?" Lucien said.

"What man isn't?" Warren added. "To work with your hands all your life, to labor, grow things and suddenly you can't anymore? The notion gives me the shivers."

"Working in a bank is different in that respect," Lucien said. "Less physical, more mental—just as tiring, but in a different fashion. I look forward to the day I no longer have to labor in such a manner."

"What do you look forward to?" Billie asked, curious.

He grinned. "To travel the world with you, if I have my way."

A surprised gasp escaped her.

"Travel?" Bernice said with a sigh. "That sounds wonderful."

"Don't get my wife started," Warren groaned playfully.

"Hush, you," Bernice teased and stood. "The water should be ready. Billie, would you like to help me?"

She nodded, then looked at Lucien, who smiled and winked. Blushing, she rose and followed Bernice into the kitchen.

"I must admit, I'm jealous," Bernice said as she

grabbed a rag and took the kettle off the stove. She poured water into the teapot, returned the kettle and reached for a plate of fresh-baked cookies. "I've always dreamed of traveling. That was one of the reasons I became a mail-order bride."

"Really?" Billie said, eyebrows raised in curiosity.

"Yes, though I didn't travel far. I'm from a town in Oregon called Independence. I didn't cross the nation, let alone the ocean, like you did. I love your accent, by the way."

Billie smiled. "Thank you. I did travel a bit to get here, I suppose."

"Suppose?" Bernice said with a laugh. "I've *dreamed* of going abroad. And here you've already done it. You'll have to tell me all about England."

"All right," Billie said. "And you can tell me all about Oregon."

Bernice laughed as she set cups and saucers on a tray. "I'm afraid there's not much to tell, though I have a few amusing stories."

"There seems to be no end of those around here. I've heard several already."

"You'll hear a lot more. Help me carry this into the parlor." She nodded at the plate of cookies.

When they rejoined the men, Bernice poured while Billie passed out cookies. The four chatted companionably for a time, before being joined by the elder Johnson. "What's all the ruckus down here?" he said roughly before catching sight of Billie. "Jumpin' Jehoshaphat—howdy!" He went straight to her and held out his hand. "I'm Grandpa Johnson, who're you?"

Bernice hid her face in her hands. "Grandpa," she groaned.

"Grandpa what?" he snapped. "Ain't anyone gonna introduce me?"

Warren stood and guided his grandfather to a chair. "Here, sit and I'll pour you a cup of tea. You know Lucien from the bank?"

Grandpa Johnson peered at Lucien over his spectacles. "Howdy. You're lookin' good, young man."

"Thank you. I'm glad to see you up and around."

"And I'm glad I can open my eyes in the mornin'," he shot back, then looked Billie up and down. "And what about you, young lady? You look the adventurous type."

She giggled in response as Lucien joined her on the loveseat. "Mr. Johnson, my betrothed, Miss Billie Jane Sneed. And yes, she's had her share of adventures, and is looking forward to a whole new set of them with me." He took her hand. "Aren't you, sweetheart?"

His hand was big and warm, and she reveled in the feel of it. He was protecting her, changing the subject so she wouldn't have to talk about her scars or lost eye. She smiled. "Yes, I am."

"And for our first adventure," Lucien said, "we're joining you for supper."

"Yippee!" Grandpa Johnson cried. "Won't that be somethin'?"

Bernice and Warren laughed. "Yes, it will," Bernice said. "And as soon as we finish our tea, Billie can help me in the kitchen."

Billie nodded without thinking. She was comfortable around these people and liked Warren's grandfather. She watched him take a cup and saucer from his grandson, followed by a cookie. His eyes twinkled as he dunked it in his tea.

"Billie, are you finished?" Bernice asked as she stood.

"Yes." With a pang of regret, she pulled her hand from Lucien's. "I'll go help her," she told him.

"Enjoy yourselves." He leaned toward her and quietly added, "I'll miss you while you're gone."

Billie blushed fiercely, shivering as she stood.

Bernice gave her a knowing look before turning to Grandpa. "Behave yourself."

"Me? Always!"

Bernice snorted, took Billie by the hand and led her into the kitchen.

"Lucien is a good man," Bernice said as she brought a bowl of raw potatoes to the table. "You're a lucky woman."

Billie's spine tingled. "Yes, he is a good man." *Too good for me.* She shook her head and tried to push the thought from her mind.

"Is something wrong?" Bernice asked.

"Nothing," she said with a shrug.

Bernice sat, a paring knife in her hand. "If we both peel, we'll get them done in no time." She slid a second knife across the table.

Billie sat and picked it up. "Hand me a few," she said with a nod at the bowl.

Bernice gave her three. "Do they hurt?" She looked at Billie, her face full of compassion. "I don't mean to pry, but I can't help but notice your scars are new."

"No." Billy touched her cheek. "Funny, it didn't hurt at the time. Later, though…"

"I can imagine… I'm sorry, I'm being nosy."

"Hard not to be," Billie said with a smile. "I was attacked protecting my father."

"You don't have to tell me any more." Bernice began to peel a potato.

"I'd like to tell it if you don't mind. Better you hear it from me than secondhand from someone in town."

Bernice rolled her eyes. "Like Nellie Davis, for example."

"I was thinking Mrs. Ferguson, actually," Billie admitted. "I've heard the stories about Mrs. Davis, but I've spent time with the woman and I think she's trying to mend her ways."

"Thank the Lord for that," Bernice said. "She and my mother make quite a team. If Nellie rehabilitates herself, then…" She shook her head. "…well, maybe there's hope."

"For your mother?"

Bernice nodded. "She's horrible—always has been. Warren and I used to joke who was the worse busybody, her or Nellie. You're lucky Lucien's parents live far away—though actually, they might be very nice, I don't know."

"Is your mother here in Nowhere?"

"Thank heavens, no," Bernice said with a giggle. "Don't get me wrong, I love her, but she's a lot easier to love when she's in another state."

Billie peeled potatoes as her words sunk in. She might be disfigured and unpleasant to look at on the outside, but her father had loved her dearly. She couldn't imagine what it would be like to have one's parent be her tormentor.

"I hope you like fried chicken," Bernice said, breaking into her thoughts.

"I've tried it, but only once. I'm curious how to make it."

Bernice's eyes popped. "You've never made fried chicken?"

Billie shook her head. "Alas, my life has lent itself to more adventure than recipes."

"Then you've come to the right place. I got the most wonderful recipe from Elle Riley. They live on the other side of our orchards."

"Yes, I heard you were neighbors."

Bernice reached for another potato. "When I first came here I was so…well, it wasn't pretty. And neither was I. Elle helped me a lot."

Billie stared at her. True, the woman was cadaverously thin, but she was sweet and kind—anyone could see that. And of course, she wasn't missing an eye or facially scarred.

"I was so awkward," Bernice continued. "I could hardly walk ten feet without falling on my face. And did a few times, with Warren watching."

Billie gasped.

"It's true," Bernice said. "I was the ugly duckling from the fairytales—clumsy, inept, far from beautiful."

Billie peeled as she listened. Was Bernice telling her this to make her feel better, or just recollecting?

"I couldn't cook, I couldn't sew, I'd never worked a day in my life—worthless." She rolled her eyes. "Now here I am, married to the most wonderful man in the world. He saw so much in me that I couldn't."

Billie set down the knife. "And you're telling me this because…?"

Bernice smiled. "Because you remind me of me. I know that sounds silly, but that's what I sense—that you feel awkward, and maybe don't see your own worth. I just felt it had to be said."

Billie closed her mouth, having just realized it was hanging open. How had the girl known? "Thank you."

Bernice nodded. "You're welcome. Now let's finish these potatoes, and I'll show you how I fry chicken."

Lucien made a fist. "I'm telling you, if I ever get my hands on the man who harmed her, I'll…"

"Killin' the man ain't the answer," Warren's grandfather cut in. "Killin' don't solve nothin'."

Lucien released a long breath. "I was going to say the more general 'make sure he pays,' and I don't think I could kill a man in cold blood. But I take your point."

"Only natural you'd be angry," Grandpa said. "She's your bride. Don't make no difference it happened 'fore you met her. She's an innocent woman that was attacked and lost her pa. Makes me want to shoot the snake myself."

"Me too," Warren said. "And thank you for telling us what happened. Poor thing. I hope she comes to visit again. I remember how Bernice was when she first arrived."

"I heard she had her moments."

"Like gettin' sprayed by a skunk?" Grandpa said with a laugh. "Now that was somethin'!"

"Grandpa!" Warren said, then chuckled. "It wasn't funny at the time. Took poor Bernice three weeks to get rid of the stink."

Lucien chuckled too. He'd heard stories of Warren and Bernice's hazardous courtship from Spencer Riley. "The last thing my bride—or I—need is a run-in with a skunk."

Warren and his grandfather laughed. Then Grandpa's eyes lit up. "Hey, that's an idea!"

"What?" Warren asked.

He looked at Lucien. "Why don't you get hitched here on the farm? Daniel Weaver got married in one of their orchards. You could do the same. That way there's plenty of room for folks that want to come."

Lucien exchanged a quick look with Warren. "Here on your farm?"

"Why not?" Warren said. "There's already been talk about a town picnic. But if that's too many people…"

"Great Scott, I can't subject Billie to a public wedding at a town picnic!"

"But it's private, it's pretty, it's…" Grandpa added a wink. "…ro-man-tic."

Lucien smiled. "You sly dog."

Grandpa grinned, then sobered. "You're a good man, Lucien Miller, marryin' that gal."

"She's the bride I sent for—of course I'm going to marry her. And for the record, even if I hadn't sent away for her and she lived here in Nowhere, I'd *still* marry her. She's beyond my wildest dreams for a wife."

Warren and his grandfather exchanged a look. "Grandpa didn't mean it like that…"

"I meant it just like that." Grandpa studied Lucien. "She ain't much to look at—"

"On that, we disagree," Lucien replied, frowning.

"Well, okay. You really do like this woman, don't you? You ain't just doing it out of obligation?"

"Not in the least. The second I saw her I rejoiced and was exceedingly glad. And I'll hear no more about that, thank you. I want Billie to have the best wedding I can give her—she's worth it."

"That's not pity, Grandpa," Warren added. "He's got real feelings for her. Just like I do for Bernice." He turned to Lucien. "Congratulations on finding the woman of your dreams, friend."

"Thank you, Warren—I'm glad someone understands." Lucien abruptly stood and began pacing. "Why do so many people question my desire to marry this woman? Just because she isn't perfect to them doesn't mean she isn't perfect to me. It certainly doesn't mean she should be refused love, simply because she doesn't look like the Riley women or, or Isabella Weaver."

Warren nodded. "You're right. People assume." He glanced at his grandfather, who was looking appropriately chastened.

"Exactly. They assume that because she's not what they consider pretty, she's to be discarded. Well, I for one like a tall woman, a strong woman, an adventurous woman—and yes, a woman with a blue pinstriped eyepatch! Did anyone stop to think about that? Warren, you're the first person who's grasped that, and I thank you for it. But that it keeps coming up bothers me to no foreseeable end."

Warren nodded and glanced at the kitchen door. "As I suppose it should. Bernice is beautiful in my eyes, inside and out, and anyone who says otherwise better be prepared to answer for it."

"As Billie is to me," Lucien said. He sighed. "I just wish I could convince other people of it. Her, first and foremost."

Chapter Fourteen

Billie sat on the wagon seat, her hands in her lap, and wondered at Lucien's smile. Their evening with Bernice and Warren was pleasant, and she wanted to do it again. But wasn't confident there would be a chance to. He said he wanted to marry her. He said lots of very nice things. But…

"Do you cook?" Lucien asked, breaking into her thoughts.

She glanced at him and cringed. Yes, she could cook, but his idea of cooking and hers might be very different. "A little. Good enough for my father."

"I'm not picky, Billie," he said with a smile. "I admit I don't cook very well. Though I've avoided killing myself."

She laughed. "That is good news."

Lucien chuckled and scooted an inch toward her. "I'm glad you had a good time tonight. Bernice did too. I'm happy you made another friend, Billie. I want you to have lots of friends." He scooted closer. "But I hope to be your best friend."

"You do?" she said, her voice low. She picked at her skirt. "Are you saying you want a wife or a friend?"

"What kind of a question is that? Both, of course." To her surprise, he put his arm around her. "You're going to be my wife, but I also want you to be my friend, someone I can tell anything to."

"I thought that's what a man did with a wife," she said with a raised eyebrow.

"Yes, but…oh dear, I'm not explaining this well. Let me try again. A lot of men think of a wife as just someone who cooks and cleans and produces children. Serving a function…"

"Like a crew?" she interjected. His arm was warm against her and she fought the urge to rest her head on his shoulder. But she still wasn't sure she dared.

"Sort of, yes. But a captain doesn't marry his crew. I want to be more than that, sweetheart. And I want you to know that I don't think of you as just crew." He looked into her eyes.

Billie swallowed. She didn't know what to say, and didn't really know what he was saying. Was he talking about love, or something else? In England, arranged marriages were still common, and she'd supposed being a mail-order bride wasn't much different. You either learned to love each other or you didn't. Those that didn't took mistresses…wait, was *that* what he was trying to say? He wanted to be friends but not lovers? Or… "You'd better explain further."

"All right. What I'm trying to say is, I want to share everything with you, Billie. Not just a house and meals and a bed. I want to share my time, my life, my hopes and dreams." He looked deeply into her eyes. "And I hope you want to share all those things with me. What you want to do in your old age, how many children you want us to have…"

"Children!" she said in surprise.

"You do want them, don't you?"

"Well… I hadn't given it much thought."

"That's all right," he said with a smile. "We have plenty of time to think about it. I'm in no rush—are you?"

"No." Because she hadn't really thought she'd be getting married. Now that she knew he wasn't sending her away immediately, she really needed to rethink things.

She had the sudden urge to take off her eyepatch, let him see her without it. But she was still afraid of what he'd do. All his fine-sounding promises might vanish, and she'd lose everything all over again—him, Nowhere, Bernice, Charlotte, you name it. He'd pack her up and send her off before she could blink. She wanted her time in Nowhere to last a little longer— better hold off.

But she knew she was just stalling. It's not like she would wear her eyepatch to bed. Sooner or later, he'd have to see. And she knew it had to happen before Saturday—she didn't think she could bear him reeling away in disgust on their wedding night.

"You're suddenly quiet," he commented.

She stared at the road ahead. "I have nothing to say."

His hand touched her chin and turned her face toward his. A kiss followed, a gentle, stirring kiss that made her stomach flutter. She wasn't expecting it and didn't know what to do.

When Lucien broke it, he looked at her and smiled. "Billie, I know there's something still bothering you.

And I can hazard a guess as to what. I want you to trust me, sweetheart. Can you do that?"

Fear washed over her like a hurricane wave. She might as well get this over with. "Lucien, I can't," she said with a shake of her head.

"You can't…can't what?"

"Marry you."

"What?!"

"Don't you see? This isn't going to work. *I'm* not going to work for you. You're the one that hasn't figured it out yet."

Lucien pulled on the lines, bringing the horse to a stop. "See here, Billie, you can't assume something like that. You have no idea how I feel about you." He blinked a few times. "Well, you *should* have a good inkling by now. If you don't, then you need to take a second look."

"And *you* need to look at *this*!" Throwing caution to the wind in her frustration, she pulled off her eyepatch.

He stared, just like anyone would. But he didn't flinch, or make a face. He didn't even gasp in shock. His eyebrows went up…and slowly went back down again.

Billie sat and waited, then waited some more. "Well?"

Slowly, Lucien reached out and ran a finger over the scar above the eye, then traced the one below it down her cheek. She trembled at his touch, speechless. He leaned forward, stroked them again…and then did something she never would've expected.

He leaned closer and, gently as a feather, kissed the empty eyelid.

She couldn't pull away, couldn't move at all. His tenderness had broken something in her, the something that had driven her away from so much she wanted. Now all she could do was sit there as tears streamed from both eye sockets unchecked.

Lucien put his arms around her and pulled her against him. "Why do you fight what you are, Billie?"

"I don't know what you mean," she mumbled into his shoulder.

"Billie…you're beautiful!" He kissed her lips then, gently but firmly. It was all she had ever dreamed of, but still her heart drew back. How could he say such things? She was no beauty and she knew it. Why torture her like this? She tried to pull away.

Lucien broke the kiss. "Billie, don't."

"Let me go!" She continued to squirm.

"No."

She stared at him and blinked. "What?"

He laughed. "Pay attention, you silly woman! I'm trying to show how I feel about you. What does a man have to do?"

"Feel about me?" she said, shaking her head. Was he serious?

He nodded. "Yes!"

Egads, he *was* serious! She opened and closed her mouth a few times, but had no words. She could understand a small show of affection, a peck on the cheek maybe. But this…

"You don't give yourself enough credit." He released her.

She quickly scooted to the other side of the seat. "I don't know what you mean."

"I know," he said dourly. "But I'll keep explaining until you do."

She looked at him. "Why are you toying with me?"

He sighed. "I'm not. I'm trying to give you a taste of what's to come."

"You're talking about our wedding…"

"I'm talking about our *marriage*," he corrected. "A wedding is just one day. A marriage is a lifetime."

She stared at him in disbelief as more tears rolled down her cheeks.

He reached over and wiped them away with his thumb. "Let me show you, Billie. Don't be afraid to open your heart to me. Let me in and I'll show you things you've never dreamed of." He paused, then added, "I love you, Billie Jane Sneed. *You're* the one that hasn't figured it out yet."

She swallowed hard. His declaration of love, combined with use of her words, hit her amidships. What to do? She never experienced anything like this. He couldn't possibly be in love—it was too soon for that. And in love with her?! How could he be?

But one thing she knew about Lucien Miller was that he was no liar. Deluded, maybe. But he wasn't trying to deceive her.

The truth was, she liked him too, and thought she could fall in love with him if she dared. She wanted to believe his words, but they were just that—words.

But what about his actions? her mind asked. *What are you going to do about those?*

Billie closed her eye against the voice. She didn't want to hear it, didn't want to think about the answer. She was still too scared.

She didn't want to be afraid. But she couldn't seem to stop.

* * *

Lucien took up the lines and gave the horses a slap. The buggy lurched forward as they broke into a trot. He'd scared her, he knew. But he had to make her understand not only how he felt about her, but how she felt about herself. How could she love him if she didn't love herself first? It was a principle his mother had taught him years ago and he'd never forgotten it.

He sighed. This might be harder than he'd thought. But he always did like a challenge, and winning Billie's heart was worth it. He let the silence stretch for a few minutes before he broke it. "The town picnic is next week."

She'd been staring at the road again and looked at him. "It is?"

"Yes. You plan to attend, don't you?"

She looked away again. "What day is it?"

"A week from Saturday. Are you having a wedding dress made?"

"Er, yes," she blurted.

Lucien looked at her. "Have you talked to Betsy and Charlotte?" He knew this was a conversation they'd already had, but to make her feel comfortable he'd give it another go.

"I need to speak with them again." She folded her hands in her lap, eye on the road once more. "The question is, do I need one?"

"Yes, if that's what you want."

"Is that what *you* want?"

"Billie, don't make me stop this buggy again. I want to marry you. The only person that can stop me from doing it is you. And you're here as my mail-order bride—if you didn't want to get married, why did you come?" Good heavens, he was angry. No—frustrated. Why couldn't she accept that he loved her?

"My father. He wanted me to marry."

Lucien glanced between her and the road. "He... did?" Good grief, where did that leave them?

"It was his dying wish," she said with little emotion. "Didn't I mention that?"

"Not to me." He yanked the lines and brought the horse to a stop again. When he turned to her his jaw was tight. He wanted to take her in his arms and kiss her senseless, the stubborn fool. "Let me get this straight. The only reason you became a mail-order bride was to honor a promise to your father?"

She swallowed hard and nodded.

"So what do *you* want?"

"What?" she repeated with a raised eyebrow. "Does it matter?"

"Yes, it matters!" he said. "We're talking about the rest of your life, Billie."

She picked at her skirt. "I...hadn't put that much thought into it."

Lucien groaned. "Great Scott, woman, this is your life we're talking about. It's honorable that you would want to do as your father asked, but not when you're not ready for it."

"I'll never be ready, Lucien. Because I don't expect anyone to..."

"Don't you dare say it."

She snapped her mouth shut.

Lucien took a deep breath and let it out, trying to calm himself. "Billie, when you stepped off that stage, I fell irrevocably for you. You might not believe it now, but it's still the gospel truth." He stared at her, waiting for a response, this time not caring if he'd scared the wadding out of her.

She quickly looked away, as if frightened by her own thoughts.

He knew darn well what those thoughts were. And this time, he wasn't going to tolerate them. He scooted across the seat, wrapped his arms around her and pulled her close. "You silly woman. What do I have to do to get it through your head?" He kissed her, but not gently as before. No, this was a kiss meant to claim her, *all* of her.

She surprised him—she didn't struggle or try to squirm away. Instead, she even relaxed a notch. This only served to ignite his determination to show her how he felt, that his affections were sincere, that he loved her and wanted to marry her.

When Lucien finally broke the kiss she gasped and looked at him in wonder. "Lucien," she managed.

He smiled and cupped her face with one hand. "Are you convinced yet?" he asked.

She shook her head. "I'm sorry, so sorry…"

"What?" he asked gently.

"I can't help myself," she said. "I've never met a man like you before. I…don't know what to do. I want to believe you, but…"

He held her close for a moment, resting his head on hers. "I think I see. 'Love bade me welcome, but my soul drew back'…"

"Quite," she sighed. "Is that from a poem?"

"Yes, it is—Gerard Manley Hopkins. But you don't have to do anything, sweetheart, except let your heart go."

She shook her head. "I don't know how."

"That's okay, honey, I do. I'll teach you."

She pulled away to look at him. "Teach me?"

Lucien nodded. "Yes, but I must warn you, it won't be easy." His words would frighten her, he knew, but she had to know the truth. Getting past one's greatest fears never was easy. He could sense Billie's fear that no one could love her, and he was ready to do whatever was necessary to prove her wrong.

Chapter Fifteen

Billie trudged up the stairs to her room after Lucien dropped her in front of the hotel. He'd have escorted her inside, but he had to return the buggy to the livery stable. Due to all their stopping and starting on the way back to town, they were late.

A blessing in disguise, really—she didn't think she could stand another kiss from him. The ones he'd given made her heart melt and her head swim and she wasn't sure she could feel her toes at one point. Who knew a simple kiss could do such things?

She got ready for bed, pulled out her book and read until she could read no more. She wanted to sleep and not dream, afraid she'd dream of nothing but Lucien. She was confused and felt out of control, and that made her want to flee and not look back. But eventually she dropped off into a mercifully dreamless slumber.

The next morning she went through her normal routine and once ready, stood and stared at the door. Lucien had told her yesterday he had things to do at the bank this morning and he'd show her his house afterwards. Did she really want to see it? Wouldn't that add to her conflicting emotions? He made her want to stay, to get married. But what if he just thought he was doing the noble thing? If that were the case, then she needed to put a stop to this before it was too late. *Before* they married.

Once in a state of matrimony, he was too honorable to back out. Then in time he'd take a mistress, because she wasn't attractive enough. He might like her. He might even love her. But how could he possibly *be in love* with her? He couldn't...

...Could he?

Before she knew it, she found herself at Hank's restaurant, ordering breakfast. "You look like you haven't slept for a week," Nellie commented as she poured her coffee. "What's the matter?"

"Nothing. Just tired."

Nellie put a hand on her hip. "Liar."

Billie gasped and looked at her.

"You heard me. I know a liar when I see one—Lord knows I've had my share of fibs over the years. You want to talk about it?"

"No."

"That tells me you *need* to talk about it," Nellie said with an arched eyebrow. "Charlotte's having tea again this afternoon. You should come."

Billie nodded but said nothing, and Nellie turned and marched back to the kitchen with her order. If the matron could read her, what would Lucien do when he saw her? Would he sense she was ready to leave? Because if she didn't, they'd be in a heap of trouble, trapped in a marriage he wouldn't want in the long run. She'd be saving them both a lot of heartache.

She ate slowly and tried not to look at the other patrons. She could feel them staring, but not like some had in other places, thank Heaven for that. No matter—once Lucien came to his senses, she'd be gone in a day or two, head for the coast and…

"There you are," Lucien said as he plopped himself in the chair opposite her.

Billie's head snapped up. "What are you doing here?"

"I came in for a cup of coffee. I got my work done and thought I might find you here."

"You're done already?"

"Everything went much faster than I expected. Have you eaten yet?"

"Nellie just took my plate away."

"Fine, I'll pay your bill and we can be on our way."

"What about your coffee?"

"I'll make some at my place." He glanced around, spotted Nellie and waved her to their table. "May I have Miss Sneed's bill, please?"

Nellie reached into her apron pocket, pulled out her notepad and tore off a page. "Here," she said flatly.

Lucien cocked his head. "What's the matter?"

"Well, if you must know, you need to keep your betrothed on a better schedule. You're wearing her out, Lucien Miller, traipsing off to the Johnson farm yesterday and returning the buggy late."

Lucien and Billie exchanged a quick look. "How do you know that?" he asked.

Nellie gave him a look. "You know I know everything in this town."

Billie laughed. It felt good. Lucien did as well. Even Nellie cracked a smile. "Well," Lucien drawled. "It can't be said that Nellie isn't well-informed."

"Dang skippy." She turned and left the table.

Lucien smiled at Billie. "Ready?"

She left the table, deciding she'd speak with him at his home. They'd be alone as far she knew, no witnesses to the exchange if it got heated. He was determined to prove he cared for her, but surely he was confusing affection with duty, honor or obligation. She wasn't sure which, but she had to set him to rights while there was still time.

They left Hank's and headed across town, the same direction they'd traveled the day before. "Where is your house?" she asked.

"Actually, we drove by it twice yesterday," he confessed.

"We did?" Billie's brow furrowed. "I didn't pay much attention to the houses as we went."

"Excellent. Then it will still be a surprise."

They walked arm in arm and Billie realized she hadn't noticed him take hers and wrap it through his. Maybe she'd grown used to the action. A mistake she could ill afford.

He escorted her to the last house at the edge of town. "Well, this is it."

The house was a modest whitewashed two-story structure with a porch. A white picket fence bordered the front. There was a gate in the center with a small arbor, and the front walk was paved with bricks. The whole place looked very new and very neat. "When did you build this?"

"In the last year. How did you know I built it?"

"Because it's so…organized."

He opened the gate and led her to the porch. "I do like to be organized. I'm glad you noticed." He took a key out of his pocket and unlocked the front door. "After you." He motioned her inside.

Billie preceded him into the parlor and took a breath. It was beautiful. The furniture was new and of the latest style, as were the fixtures. The wallpaper was cream-colored with tiny flowers, and the dining room beyond matched.

"Well, what do you think?" he asked with a grin.

"It's lovely." She turned to him. "Are you sure you didn't have help decorating?"

"None, except for a few things Charlotte suggested."

"Everything is beautiful, Lucien, it truly is."

Lucien came closer, took her hands and gave them a squeeze. "It's yours." Billie tried to take a step back, but he held fast. "Don't," he said softly, leaned forward and kissed her gently on the cheek. "All of it, Billie. All of this is yours."

She shut her eye tight, as if that would keep his words at bay. "Lucien…" She opened it. "There are so many other women…"

"That don't compare to you," he finished.

Her heart melted. She couldn't keep her resistance up—the man was slowly but surely making it crumble. If he succeeded, he'd reach her heart, and what then?

"Come, I'll show you the kitchen." He gave her hands a tug.

She nodded as he led her into the dining room. He stopped, let her look around, then pulled her through a door into the next room. "Here we are."

Like the rest of the house, it was neat and charming, and big enough for a decent feast. What bride wouldn't be pleased? She swallowed hard. "How many bedrooms?"

"Just two. If we need more, we can add on." He

opened a nearby hutch, pulled out a jar of coffee and held it up. "Do you want some?"

She could use something stronger than coffee, but she doubted he'd have any gin around. "Yes, please."

He busied himself preparing the pot and putting it on the stove. "We're lucky I banked the fire. Otherwise I'd have to start a new one."

She smiled weakly and studied the kitchen some more. It had a sink with a water pump and she sighed. "You have indoor plumbing?"

"Yes," he said proudly. "The house might be small, but I spared no expense on some things, plumbing being one of them. It does get cold here in the winter, and I didn't fancy my future bride having to trudge to an outhouse in several feet of snow. Wait until you see the water closet upstairs."

"You have a water closet?" she said in surprise.

"Yes, and a bathtub with its own pump here on the first floor."

She backed into the nearest chair and sat. He seemed to have thought of everything. What woman didn't want indoor plumbing? She knew it was expensive, though. "So that's why you had to build a small house?"

"No, I could have built a larger one. It's not that I couldn't afford it. But what would I need all that space for?"

She nodded in understanding. Lucien was practical, not spendthrift. He was everything a woman could want—which was precisely the problem. The man was simply too good to be true, especially for the likes of her. Why would he settle for...?

If you were living in ancient Rome or Greece, they would have built temples to you...the words wafted back into her mind unbidden. It sounded like mummery—it couldn't really be how he felt. But…

"Come, Billie, I want to show you something." He motioned her back into the dining room. She followed him to a china cabinet, which he pointed at and smiled. He opened it and pulled out a plate. "Charlotte picked these out. This is the set I told you about the other day." He handed her the plate.

She took it with care. It was red and white with a beautiful pattern of poppies. "She's right. What woman wouldn't love this?"

"Do you want to change the curtains?"

Billie looked at the solid blue velvet, which offset the wallpaper nicely. "In truth, I wouldn't change a thing."

"I'm glad." He took her in his arms.

She stiffened, caught herself and tried to relax. Now was the time. "Lucien…"

"No, don't speak." He tucked a finger under her chin, lifted her face and kissed her. "Now, I know we're alone and un-chaperoned, so perhaps I shouldn't have done that."

A laugh escaped her. "And what about yesterday? Not to mention a few moments ago?"

"I admit, I am behaving less than a gentleman, but I believe my actions are necessary—a display of affection to reiterate my feelings toward you, and to convince you that you're doing the right thing."

"By coming here? Or honoring my father's dying wish?"

"Both," he said. "You belong here, Billie. You belong with me."

She sighed wearily. "Lucien, not this again."

"Yes, this again—and again and again, until it gets

through that fortress you've built around your heart, my dear."

She looked at him, a tear in her eye. "Why?" she asked in a small voice. "Why are you being so kind to me?"

He pulled her closer. "Because to me, you are more wonderful than any woman I've ever met or ever hoped to. I see great strength in you, a strength I wish I had. I don't know how I would have handled what you endured. I'd probably be in jail or a sanatorium."

"You're a man," she said. "You could have saved yourself from what happened to me. I barely survived."

"But that's just it—you did survive, and admirably. I don't want some wilting flower for a wife, Billie. I've always desired a strong woman. And you, my dear, are strong." He cupped her face with one hand. "And more beautiful than you know."

She let her eye drift to the dining table. "No one has ever spoken to me this way."

"I should hope not, or you'd be married to them."

She smiled stiffly. "You are determined."

"To marry you? By God and all His angels, woman, isn't it obvious?"

"Very," she said. "But if I'm to be honest, I still think I'll disappoint you." There, she'd said it. Her heart was beating so hard now she felt as if it would burst from her chest, fortress or no fortress.

"Billie, look at me. What do you see?"

She looked at him, right in the eyes, and did her best not to cry. He was tearing down her walls, breaking through her fear. It was foreign and uncomfortable and it scared her senseless. She had a sudden thought, wondering what would happen if she let him...but that was too dangerous. "I see a very handsome man who's being incredibly kind to me. Generous. Open-hearted."

"Open-hearted?" he said with a raised eyebrow. "I like that. Well, what you see is what you get."

Her eyebrows rose with curiosity.

"And what I see is what I get. Right now I see a woman who doesn't believe anyone can love her."

She looked away.

"Bold words, I know. They might sting, but they have to be said. In time I know that will change."

"To what?"

He smiled. "To a woman who does believe. To a woman who can receive love, and does."

Billie bit her lip. She wanted that to happen. Love bade her welcome, indeed—but would her soul ever stop drawing back?

Billie sat in her room and stared out the window at the street below. What was this man doing to her? At first it was only his kisses that made her head swim and her heart melt. Now it was his words. Lucien Miller was going to be the death of her—or scarier, the life of her. She got up, crossed the room and hugged herself.

When she returned to the window, she saw Charlotte Quinn enter the hotel from the street below and remembered Nellie's mention of tea. Maybe she was coming to invite her. But did she want tea and friendship now? She felt so shaken, already on the verge of tears. How could she face them? It was all the fault of Lucien's words and actions. Bollocks, what was this man doing to her?

A soft knock on the door drew her attention. She

took a deep breath and answered it. "Hello," she said, calmer than she felt.

"Hello," Charlotte replied. "My mother informed me she told you about this afternoon. Did you want to come?"

"I don't know." Billie turned away, unable to face her friend.

Charlotte followed her into the room. "Billie, what's wrong?"

"Nothing. Everything."

Charlotte immediately took her in her arms. "What is it? You and Lucien didn't have a fight, did you?"

"No. Well, a little. But I was the only one fighting."

"What?" Charlotte stood back. "I want to hear this."

Billie rubbed her temples. "I'm not sure I want to tell it."

"You're still getting married, aren't you?"

Billie put some distance between them and hugged herself again. "I don't know. I don't know anything anymore."

Charlotte followed her and put her hands on her shoulders. "Billie, you're not making sense."

"I know. But this whole day hasn't made sense. And neither did yesterday…" She waved a hand at the window. "I don't even want to try to explain yesterday."

Charlotte walked over to the settee, sat and patted it in invitation. "Let's talk."

"Do we have to?"

"I think it's for the best. Besides, if something's going on, you have to get it off your chest."

"I suppose." Billie came over and sat. "Lucien Miller is a wonderful man."

"Anyone in town can tell you that. So what's the problem?"

"He thinks I'm wonderful too."

Charlotte arched an eyebrow. "And?"

Billie clasped her hands together and tried not to wring them. "He wants to marry me."

"I should hope so, considering he sent away for you for just that purpose," Charlotte pointed out. "Oh dear... don't tell me you don't want to marry him?"

Billie didn't bother to hold back her tears. "That's just it, I do want to!"

Chapter Sixteen

Charlotte marched into the mercantile, Billie on her arm. "Ladies! We have a bridal emergency!"

At the counter, Leona Riley whipped around with a swirl of skirts. "We do?"

Betsy Quinn, on the other side of the counter, clapped her hands. "Thank the Lord!"

"No time for celebration," Charlotte barked. "When I say emergency, I mean *emergency*!"

Betsy hurried around the counter to join Leona. "What's the matter?"

"Billie has cold feet—we need to heat them up."

Betsy and Leona exchanged a quick look. "You can count on us," Leona said. "After all, you wouldn't be the first bride to get the collywobbles around here."

"I'm not?" Billie said in surprise.

"Heavens, no, child," Betsy said. "Just ask Charlotte."

Charlotte shrugged. "Oh, you might as well know the whole story. I almost didn't marry Matthew."

"Yes, I heard something about that."

"What you didn't hear was that I almost married

Tom Turner, and Matthew almost married Rose. Mother Quinn had sent away for Rose, and was very opposed to me—for good reason, given how I'd been acting. Both mismatched couples were already at the altar and if Tom hadn't spoken up right then, we would've stayed mismatched for life, since my feet were cold enough to freeze my mouth shut."

Billie gasped.

"It's true," Betsy confirmed. "And Miss Sneed, you're about to marry one of the most wonderful men in town. You need to understand that."

"What?" Leona said. "Are you having misgivings about Lucien?"

"No…not exactly." Billie shut her eye tight. She might as well let them know. "It's just that I… I don't think…"

Charlotte wasn't going to wait for her. "Her head is full of nonsense that he's too good for her or some silliness like that."

Betsy and Leona shared another look. "Oh, you poor dear," Leona replied. "A case of the 'I'm not worthy' blues."

"The what?" Billie said, her eyebrow raised in curiosity.

"Yes," Leona said with a nod. "You should've seen my poor daughter-in-law Summer when she first came to town. If Clayton hadn't shot her in the foot…"

"He did what?" Billie interjected.

"It was an accident. They fell in love while she was convalescing—at least Clayton did. Summer didn't think she was good enough for him. Isn't that right, Charlotte?"

Charlotte blushed. "Yes, and Mother and I didn't

help, since I had my cap set for Clayton. I was horrible back then, and I made sure Summer felt horrible about herself. And when that didn't work, I re-set my cap for his brother Spencer, and made Elle suffer when she came to town."

Betsy nodded. "You were a hellion for a while there. That's why I was determined to keep you and Matthew apart. But you were already changing for the better—I just didn't know it yet."

"Indeed she was," Leona added. "But everything turned out for the best and my two sons are happily married to wonderful women."

"And I got a wonderful daughter-in-law," Betsy said with a smile and gave Charlotte a hug.

When they parted Billie could see tears in Charlotte's eyes. "You changed."

"Oh, my heart was black as night then, Billie. But if I can change, so can you."

"Change?" Leona said curious. "What are you talking about?"

"I'm talking about Billie wanting to marry Lucien," Charlotte said.

"What's the matter, child—don't you want to marry him?" Betsy asked, bringing them full circle.

"No, I do," Billie said. "There lies the problem."

Leona blinked a few times. "Okay, I'm confused—will one of you kindly explain to me what this is about?"

"*She* doesn't believe she deserves *him*," Charlotte stated. "Or anyone."

"All right, that's what I thought before," Leona replied.

"Well, if Charlotte, Summer and Elle could get past their fears, not to mention Bernice and a few others, then so can you," Betsy said. "Land sakes, I don't know why women think these things."

Billie stared open-mouthed at the trio. It was as if her scars didn't exist and her missing eye meant nothing. Nor did they consider her height, her proportions, her complete lack of domesticity. If she was so special, why couldn't she see herself as they did?

Leona Riley looked her up and down. "White or ivory, Betsy?"

"With her hair? White, of course." Betsy headed for a stack of fabric, grabbed a bolt and hurried back to the counter. "I wish Abbey was here—she could help."

"She'll be here in half an hour for tea," Charlotte said. "In the meantime, let's get Billie's measurements."

"Splendid idea." Betsy went behind the counter, disappeared for a moment, then hurried back with a measuring tape. "Come here, child, let's see what we've got."

Billie blushed as she remembered Maitred's attempt at measuring. Well, at least this time she didn't have her bosoms wrapped up—that would save time and embarrassment.

"I'm just curious," Leona said as she approached. "Why don't you think you're fit for Lucien?"

Billie gaped at her. "Look at me!"

Leona did. "I don't see a problem, really. Yes, you've got a few scars—that doesn't make much difference."

"How can you say that?" Though she was beginning to understand.

"Honey, around here things are different. This isn't a big fancy city with fancy folk. Out here we have to take care of each other—we don't let silly things like scars get in the way. Besides, out here on the frontier we get nicked up all the time—there just about isn't a soul in town who hasn't been shot or nipped themselves with a knife or broken their arm falling out of a tree or gotten kicked by a horse. Where did you come from?"

"England, actually."

"No, after you came here and had your little misadventure. Did you spend any time in small communities?"

Billie shook her head. After her father's death, she'd gone to Trenton, which was a good-sized city. Then Philadelphia, Cincinnati, Gary, Kansas City and Denver, substantial towns all. That was where the jobs were, until she decided to try the mail-order bridal route.

"Well, that explains it," Betsy said.

Billie sighed. "I think the only thing it explains is that Nowhere is special."

"It is, but so are a lot of places. The point is, people change and grow in a place where everyone knows everybody else. You have to, or at least make the effort." Betsy looked at Charlotte.

Charlotte nodded. "It's true—I made the choice to change. So has my mother…though it is taking her longer."

Betsy nodded. "Well, we older folks get more set in our ways," Leona replied.

Billie sighed again. "I'm not used to being around people like yourselves. I'm sorry if I'm offending you."

"Offending us?" Betsy said. "Child, you don't offend us—you're too sweet for that. Besides, you wouldn't be the first person who had an accident of some sort, then married. Who's that man in Clear Creek Harlan told us about, Leona?"

"Oh yes, Cutty!" Leona recalled. "My brother Harlan

Hughes was sheriff in Clear Creek, Oregon, for years and years. A fellow there named Cutty suffered horrible burns, plus he had a past you wouldn't believe. But he's happily married now. In fact, he and his wife are both English like you, and both got a second chance at love. They weren't as young as you when they met, either."

"Oh," Billie said, eyes wide. "Oh my." Something had shifted, something important, though she wasn't sure what. It was as if someone had blown a trumpet and the walls around her heart had fallen like Jericho's, or like a steady wind had blown up after days becalmed at sea. "Oh my…"

"Stop saying that—the suspense is killing me," Betsy said.

Billie shook her head, unable to clarify. She was still trying to figure out what was occurring herself.

"Let's get you measured, dear," Leona said, ignoring her revelations. "Then we'll decide on a few things."

Billie stood in stunned silence as the women measured her, but they didn't make any off-hand remarks, simply took her measurements and jotted them down. They moved on to picking out different bits of lace, buttons and other fripperies to adorn the dress.

By the time they were done, Abbey had arrived. "What's this?" she asked as she looked at the stack of goods on the counter. "Are we finally making your dress, Miss Sneed?"

Billie was still too stunned to speak. She felt different somehow and wondered how long it would last. There was nothing wrong with how she felt. On the contrary, she felt…right? Fixed? Healed?

"Billie?" Charlotte said with concern.

She looked at her. "Thank you."

"For what?"

Billie's jaw trembled with emotion. She went to Charlotte and flung her arms around her. "Thank you."

"What did I do?" Charlotte asked, eyes wide.

She took a step back and wiped a tear from her eye, feeling as if her emotions were pouring out like the tide. "Thank you…" They were the only words she could manage, or needed.

Charlotte shrugged. "You're welcome. I think I have an idea what you're thanking me for."

"I don't," Abbey said in confusion.

Leona smiled. "That's all right, dear, we'll fill you in later. Right now we have a dress to make."

Lucien paced to one side of the sheriff's office and back. "Nothing can be done?"

"I'm afraid not," Spencer said. "If Billie gave a description of the scoundrel to the law in New Jersey, they're the ones to take care of him," Spencer said. "Without a name, it's like finding a needle in a haystack. And we certainly can't do much about it here."

"He's right," Clayton added.

Lucien nodded. He'd happened into Spencer and Clayton in front of the sheriff's office while coming back from seeing Pastor Lewis—he'd had to tell him the wedding was being pushed back. Warren Johnson strolled by and joined the group, and the four men conversed about their wives (or in Lucien's case, wife-to-be). Then it occurred to Lucien to ask how the man that assaulted Billie and killed her father could be found.

"The thing to do now is marry the woman," Warren said. "Get her involved with the other ladies in town. Have her spend more time with Bernice if it helps. My wife didn't think I'd want her, the fool thing. She understands what Billie's going through."

"Thank you for being so understanding, Warren," Lucien said. "I appreciate it. Billie enjoyed the other night, and so did I."

"The picnic will be a fine time to introduce her to folks," Clayton said. "Be better if you could introduce her as your wife."

Lucien nodded to himself. The town picnic was a week from Saturday. If Billie wanted a wedding dress and Charlotte and Abbey worked on it, they could be married beforehand, and he could introduce her as his wife. But what if they didn't finish it, and they had to wait until after the picnic to marry? What if Billie didn't want to wed until afterwards?

"What are you thinking?" Warren asked.

"Timing," Lucien said as he paced the room.

"When you marry the gal doesn't matter," Spencer said. "Sure, it would be nice to introduce her as your wife during the picnic, but is it necessary? Marry her when she's good and ready, that's my advice."

"Sound advice," Lucien commented, but didn't stop pacing.

"As to the other matter," Clayton said, "you can't take revenge on the man who harmed your bride, but you can rescue her."

Lucien's eyebrows rose as he smiled. "I've been trying."

"Good—it'll take time, but you'll do it," Clayton said. "Speaking from experience."

"Thank you for your advice, gentlemen. I'll speak with her. Just do me a favor—if you see her trying to leave town, don't let her."

"Leave town?" Warren asked. "Why in Heaven's name would she do that?"

Lucien sighed as he put on his hat. "Because she's convinced herself she's no good for me."

Spencer smiled. "I'll do better than stop her. I'll arrest her."

Lucien laughed, shook Spencer's hand and left the sheriff's office. It was time to once again show Billie Jane Sneed he meant business.

Billie stared at her reflection as she modeled the frilly yellow day dress. Charlotte, Abbey, Betsy and Leona stood behind her. Nellie added the finishing touch, a pretty yellow hat trimmed in lace with flowers. "There, you look a vision," she said. "Mary Weaver outdid herself with that hat."

Billie reached up and touched it. The hat really was lovely—and, she had to admit, so was she. She'd never thought of herself as pretty before—passable, perhaps; average on a good day. But with these clothes and her hair done up in the latest style (compliments of Abbey), she was actually pretty for once. Well, maybe the eye-patch with the daisy on it was a bit much…but it was nice of Betsy to whip it up out of cloth scraps and a silk flower.

"Lucien will love this," Charlotte commented. "And these are ready-made clothes."

"This dress is…stunning," Billie said as she continued to stare.

"Isabella Weaver is quite the seamstress," Nellie said. "Even Mrs. Jorgenson, our local dressmaker, thinks so."

"She certainly is," Billie said as she turned this way

and that to see the back of the outfit. "Your Mrs. Jorgensen must rejoice that the woman lives out of town."

"Believe me, she does," Leona drawled. The other women giggled.

"Shall we try on another?" Abbey asked.

"No, she won't," Betsy said, hands on hips. "We need to get her wedding dress started. If we all pitch in, we can have it done in no time."

Leona grinned. "Then you can be married."

For once, the thought didn't frighten Billie. "You all have been so kind."

"It's our pleasure, dear," Leona said. "Besides, who doesn't love to try on pretty clothes for fun?"

"That dress was made for you," Betsy said with a smile. "Won't Lucien be fit to be tied when he sees you?"

Billie turned back to the mirror. "I hope so."

"Hope so?" Charlotte said. "We *know* so."

Billie hugged Charlotte again. "Thank you, thank you so much. I don't know what happened, but I... I feel different."

"It's called confidence," Nellie replied. "Have enough confidence and you can do anything—right, Charlotte?"

Charlotte rolled her eyes, then smiled. "Yes, but watch how you use it. Take it from us, we were masters at using it to get what we wanted."

"Were?" Nellie said. "Speak for yourself, dear daughter—I've still got a ways to go."

"Nellie, don't start," Leona said. "Billie gets the idea, don't you, dear?"

Billie looked at each of them in turn and nodded.

"I'm beginning to. I... I've never had friends like you before."

"You've never lived in a small town before either, from the sounds of it," Betsy said. "Until you arrived, Lucien Miller was our most eligible bachelor—and this town doesn't have any eligible females. That's why he had to send away for a mail-order bride to find the woman who was right for him. And you *are* right for him."

Billie turned back to the mirror, pulled off her eye-patch and stared. "That's what he says too. It still seems hard to believe. But I'm beginning to."

"Good thing you didn't have to worry about competition," Nellie added.

The other women gasped. "Mother!" Abbey scolded.

Billie frowned at her reflection before turning to face them. "If a man had his choice between me and someone prettier, I'd not marry—is that what you're saying?"

Nellie sighed. "No... I didn't mean it that way..."

"Mother, enough," Abbey said. "You're confusing her."

"I was only trying to help."

"Better stop trying for now," Leona replied, taking Billie in her arms.

Nellie gritted her teeth, narrowed her eyes at Leona, then snatched up her shawl and reticule, turned on her heel and left.

"Oh, fiddlesticks," Charlotte said. "She'll be in a sour mood the rest of the week."

"And I'm staying with her," Abbey said weakly.

"Nonsense," Leona said. "She'll get over it. I think she's just mad at herself." She let go of Billie. "You'll have to excuse Nellie. She's slowly mending her ways, but sometimes she just can't help herself."

"Our mother sees things…differently," Charlotte explained, putting an arm around Abbey. "But I have to admit, she is getting better. In fact, ever since you arrived, she's been making little changes."

"But was she wrong?" Billie asked.

"In this case, yes, she was," Betsy said. "You're a wonderful girl. Maybe some other men might not find you to their liking, but Lucien isn't some other man, is he?"

"I suppose not," Billie admitted. Everything he'd said had indicated that she—tall, wide, somewhat masculine, scarred and half-blind—was pretty much his beau ideal. If he'd wanted some short, spindly girl with a heart-shaped face who could cook oysters on the half shell, he'd have sent away for one. But instead he'd sent away for her, and didn't send her back when she arrived. That said something.

"We understand, dear," Leona said. "I have two daughters-in-law who were just as unsure as you are now, only their scars were all on the inside…well, except for the bullet in Summer's foot. They healed up—it just took time."

Billie wiped at her good eye. "Thank you. Thank all of you." These women were her friends and she was quickly growing to love them—thoughts of leaving faded with every moment spent with these lovely women. Okay, so Nellie was a wild card, but she was trying to change. Shouldn't Billie do the same?

The women gathered around her and gave her a hug. In that moment, Billie felt loved. And that love was worth fighting for. It was high time she started believing what Lucien said, and let him show her how serious were his intentions. Because if she continued to fight him, she might convince him she didn't want to marry, when in truth she did. She just didn't realize how much, until she got a little help from her friends.

Chapter Seventeen

"**I**'m so glad you came to visit again," Bernice said as she took a pie out of the oven. "We'll let this cool, then see how it is after supper."

"You mean we're not going to try it before the men do?" Billie asked nervously.

Bernice set the pie on the worktable. "Don't look so worried. This is Elle Riley's recipe, and she taught me everything I know about cooking. And now I'm teaching you."

Billie sat in a chair at the kitchen table. Warren and Bernice had stopped by the hotel on their way home from getting supplies at Quinn's Mercantile and invited her to supper. When she agreed, Warren strolled to the bank and invited Lucien, who would drive her home. A thrill of excitement went up her spine at the thought. "Lucien will like it?"

"He'll love it. Land sakes, you told me this isn't your first pie."

"No, but I've not made too many. There are a lot of things I never thought to attempt. It was easier to go to a shoppe."

"None of those around here. We have to do our own baking."

"Yes, so I've heard. And Hank's baking as well."

Bernice laughed again. "Poor Hank, he's always so busy. He has to rely on the generosity of the local women to supply his restaurant. At least he pays a decent amount."

"Enough to break even?"

"Probably. Say, there's an idea—when you get good at baking, you could make a deal with him and name your price. I bet being from overseas, you know a few dishes we don't."

"Perhaps, but I don't know if my baking will be good enough for that."

Bernice put her hands on her hips. "Stop doubting yourself. You're reminding me of me."

Billie sighed. "A hard habit to break, I'm afraid."

"Don't think I don't know. I was terrible at first, always assuming the worst in every possible situation. If our places were switched, I'd have left town the moment I set eyes on Lucien."

"What? Why?"

"Look at him, Billie—he's gorgeous. I'd have quit the moment I saw him."

"But…you have nothing to hide."

"Except my inadequacy," Bernice said. "And in my eyes, I was nothing. You at least have a few things going for you. You're tall and strong, you've got fight…"

"Fight?"

Bernice sighed. "You're a survivor. Frankly, you're the type of woman Warren wanted. That's hard for me to admit."

Billie shook her head. "I don't understand."

Bernice joined her at the table and sat. "He wanted a woman like you to help him work the farm. Instead he got me."

Billie looked her over as realization dawned. Bernice was tiny, probably the last thing an apple farmer like Warren Johnson would want. "Oh yes, I see. But he loves you?"

"Of course he loves me. Despite my size and my inability to do all the things he wished I could, he doesn't complain. He fell in love with me despite what I thought."

A tiny laugh escaped Billie.

"Yes, it is rather funny, now that I think about it," Bernice said. "I don't remember who told me this— maybe it was Leona Riley. I stayed with them while Warren and I courted. She said there's someone out there for everyone. For you, it's Lucien."

Billie smiled back. "Yes, it is." Another weight suddenly lifted, as if her words released them. Perhaps they had. She smiled again. "And I'm going to marry Lucien."

"Yes, you are. Now just keep telling yourself that. Pinch your arm now and then if it helps—I did enough of it while Warren courted me."

Billie nodded, excitement gripping her heart. She was a woman, a unique one, and Lucien thought she was tremendous. She was learning that, slowly but surely. Thank the Lord he'd given her plenty of actions to go along with his words: his gazes, his kisses, his generosity and close attention to her welfare. He was a good man, and she'd have been a fool to toss him away.

She looked at Bernice and smiled. *Thank You, Lord, for showing me through my new friends that I am not alone, nor the only one with fears and troubles and self-doubts. And thank You for having Bernice make me a better cook!*

"So," Billie said. "What are we making the men for dinner?"

Lucien took another bite of pie and sighed in satisfaction. "My compliments."

Billie beamed. "Thank you."

His eyes widened. "You made this?"

"She most certainly did," Bernice cut in.

"With a little help," Billie admitted. "Not my recipe."

"Nor mine," Bernice said.

"It's not the recipe, but the hands that made it." Lucien gave Billie a wink. "It was delicious. Great Scott, but I may get fat."

Everyone at the table laughed. "Best have Billie help with the pies for the picnic," Grandpa suggested. "There's a lot of work to be done between now and then."

"I'd almost forgotten about that." Lucien gazed at Billie across the table. "There's something I've been meaning to ask. Do you want to get married after the picnic?"

She smiled at him. Once again, he was putting her wants first. "We can marry as soon as my dress is done."

"They've started then?"

She smiled and nodded as her chest warmed. Little by little, she felt herself sliding into what could only be described as a pool of tranquility. Was it love for this man, or that she was no longer fighting with herself? Billie wasn't sure. Maybe both. But she knew she was ready to let herself fall in love. If her new friends adored and trusted the man, why couldn't she?

Well, now she knew why—and that she wasn't the only one to go through such a struggle. Learning of Bernice's and other women's trials had given her a confidence she'd been lacking. She could've lost her chance at love if she'd continued on the path she'd set for herself.

"Billie?"

She looked at him. "I'm sorry, I was thinking. Yes, they've started my dress."

Lucien smiled. "Good. Then as soon as it's done, we'll wed." He glanced around the table. "Any one up for more pie?"

Billie grinned. "I'll get you another piece."

"You're a bright little bird today," Lucien commented on the drive back to town.

"Oh?" she said, feigning ignorance. She patted her hair and tried to hide a smile. A scripture ran through her mind, one she'd heard countless times, but now it branded on her heart: *And ye shall know the truth, and the truth shall make you free.* And it had.

"Yes." He gave her a sidelong glance. "You're… lighter."

"Lighter?"

He grinned. "Just what sort of dress are your friends making you?"

Friends. Billie smiled again. Charlotte, Abbey, Leona, Betsy, Bernice, Nellie…okay, maybe Nellie. "A pretty one."

"You're pretty." He leaned in her direction. "Beautiful."

Billie's cheeks flamed. "Thank you."

Lucien grinned again. He took her sleeve and gave it a playful tug. "What are you doing way over there? Join me, will you?"

"Lucien Miller, I'm not inches from you."

"Too many inches. I want my bride close to me. And don't say a word about propriety—we're alone."

"You're impossible." She blushed again and scooted closer.

"And you're beautiful."

A tiny prick of doubt stabbed her, but she slapped it aside. *He thinks I'm beautiful. That means all of me, not just one or two parts*, she thought to herself. She would have to remember that if she was to win this fight and keep on winning.

Lucien put his arm around her with a smile. "There," he said softly. "Isn't this better?"

She looked at him. *He* was beautiful. A lock of his thick dark hair fell onto his forehead, the rest curling out from under his hat. He had eyes that spoke volumes, with lashes long enough to make her jealous. His face was chiseled, his frame sinewy and muscular. And he thought *she* was beautiful? Who was she to argue?

Leona Riley was right when she'd told Bernice there was someone for everyone. She'd somehow found Lucien Miller. Which made her wonder—if she hadn't become a mail-order bride, would she still have found him? What about if her father had never made his dying wish, or had never come to America? Would she be sitting next to such a man in a rented horse and buggy driving back to a town named Nowhere? Who knew?

But she did find him. And that was all that mattered.

"You're not talking," he teased.

"I'm thinking," she whispered back.

"About what?"

She licked her lips. "About...us. As husband and wife."

"Ooh, I can hardly wait to hear this." He tightened his hold and kissed her hair. "Tell me."

She shook her head. "It's a surprise."

"I love surprises." He kissed her hair again.

Billie looked into those fabulous grey eyes of his.

Lucien stared back and kissed her mouth.

Oh Father in Heaven, Billie thought as she melted against him, *I'm falling in love.*

Billie's dress was done the night before the town picnic. She even helped with part of it, and though not as good a seamstress as her friends, no one could tell whose work was whose. It was simple yet elegant, white satin with an empire waistline. Abbey had overlaid the skirt with lace and even made her a matching eyepatch. "Ready to try it on?" Charlotte asked, holding it up.

Billie touched it, then wiped away a tear. "It's so beautiful."

"I have to agree," Charlotte said. "One of the best I've ever seen. You'll be the loveliest bride we've had in years. Here, try it on."

Billie took it, went behind a changing screen and undressed. When she stepped out from behind the screen, Charlotte took a breath. "Billie, you're gorgeous!"

Billie smiled shyly, went to the mirror and gawked at herself. "Is that truly me?"

"It sure is." Charlotte did up the few buttons in back, gave a little tug here and there, then stepped back to examine her handiwork. "Lucien is going to bust a gut when he sees you in this."

Billie laughed. "I like that expression. It's one of my favorites, along with 'tarnation'."

Charlotte smiled. "Some would say you're swearing with that word. It depends on who you're talking to."

Billie turned away from the mirror. "Oh, thank you, Charlotte, from the bottom of my heart. If there's anything I can ever do for you…"

"Don't worry, there will be. This is a small town, and you'll be living just down the street."

Billie smiled. "Yes, I will, won't I?"

"Isn't it wonderful? We can have afternoon tea together, sew together and when we both have children…" Charlotte stopped and looked away. "Well, I can watch yours for you."

Billie put a hand on her arm. "Charlotte…are you barren?"

Charlotte clasped her hands in front of her. "I don't know. I don't think so."

"Forgive my prying…is it Matthew?"

She shook her head. "I think it's just…not time for us yet, that's all. At least, that's what I keep telling myself."

Billie slowly nodded, unsure of what to say. It was a delicate subject and brought sadness to Charlotte's face. She turned back to the mirror. "Didn't Abbey say she was bringing the veil by today?"

"Yes, she should be here any minute. Now that your dress is done, are you and Lucien getting married during the picnic?"

"Good heavens, no—the day after will be fine. Besides, there's so much work still to do. Bernice will be here soon to fetch me—I'm helping her with pie production again today."

"You're very kind to do so."

Billie smiled at her before stepping behind the changing screen. "It's a kindness she's teaching me how to cook better. Lucien thinks so too."

Charlotte giggled. "We'll all help you. Poor Bernice had no skill when she first arrived—the Riley women taught her most of what she knows. I contributed a little."

"You did?" Billie said as she slipped out of the dress, thankful there weren't many buttons.

"Yes. I, um, taught her how to flirt with her husband."

Billie looked at her over the screen—not hard to do at her height. "Flirt?"

"Yes, you know, be confident around a man. Tease a little. I can teach you too."

Billie's mouth slowly fell open. "When can we start?"

"As soon as you're changed," Charlotte said with a chuckle. "At this point, I'm sure Bernice could teach you a thing or two as well."

"She can?" Billie said with a smile.

"Yes, which means it's a good thing you're spending the rest of the day with her."

Billie stopped what she was doing and caught Charlotte's eye. "No, it's a good thing the Lord sent me to Nowhere. After meeting and getting to know all of you, I don't think I'd want to live anywhere else."

Charlotte went to the screen and smiled. "I don't

think we'd know what to do if you ever left. I'm glad He sent you to us."

Billie, speechless with emotion, nodded and did her best not to let her happy tears fall.

Chapter Eighteen

"You have a gazebo!" Billie said with a smile.

"Warren built it for me a couple of summers ago," Bernice said. "Makes for a nice shady place to read."

"It's lovely," Billie commented. A small table and two chairs sat in the center of Bernice's private sanctuary. A folded quilt hung over the back of one of the chairs, a book sat on the other. "You must read here often. You left your book."

"I'm here as often as I can. Once Warren and I have children, I don't imagine I'll be able to, but who knows?"

Billie nodded. Bernice was the second woman she'd met in Nowhere who was still childless after marriage. Was it an affliction? Something in the water? Or divine providence? Would she suffer the same? She shuddered at the thought as she sat in the chair with the quilt. "What a lovely place."

"I think so." Bernice joined her, picking up her book—*The Woman in White* by Wilkie Collins. "I thought we might set up some food tables here for the picnic, but I'm not sure that'll work. The space might be too small."

Billie studied the gazebo. "I agree. Maybe under those shade trees over there?" She pointed at several large evergreens bordering the barnyard.

"We could fit a few tables in here for folks to eat, then others around it on the outside. That can be our picnic area."

Billie stood. "And the food tables wouldn't be far away. Did Warren have any ideas?"

Bernice laughed. "My husband's idea is to wait until I tell him where to put things. He likes leaving the planning to me."

"He didn't want to take charge of this?"

"Merciful heavens, no—he's too busy managing the farm. Besides, it's not that much work. The last couple of times we visited town, I asked a few ladies to get the word out about what food to bring."

"Sounds easy enough."

"Nowhere is small. We handle the town Harvest Festival the same way." Bernice studied the yard. "We could put another table over by the house for the punch and lemonade."

Billie followed her gaze. "It's shady enough. Will people bring chairs?"

"Some have volunteered to, others will bring blankets to sit on." Bernice stood. "Why don't we check on our latest batch of pies?"

Billie smiled and followed her back to the house. Once in the kitchen, they took two pies from the oven and set them on the worktable. "Is this it for the day?" Billie asked.

"Yes. I thought we might relax a little before we

make supper. Are you looking forward to seeing Lucien?"

Billie blushed. "Yes, I am. I'm getting excited about the wedding too."

"So am I, and I'm not the one getting married," Bernice said with a giggle. "I'm glad you're finally excited. A week ago I would have sworn you didn't want to get married."

"Why do you say that?"

"Your eyes," Bernice said then smiled. "All right, your *eye*…"

A remark like that would have made her gut tighten before. Now she saw the humor in it. "You should've seen me when I had two. Father said he always knew what I was thinking."

"And he was right," Bernice said as she closed the oven door. "I've gotten good at reading people over the years. Some speak to you with ulterior motives. You have to know the difference."

"Are you talking about Nellie Davis?"

"Actually, I'm talking about my mother. I got a lot of practice reading people by studying my own family. But I hear she's getting better."

Grandpa entered the kitchen before Billie could comment and went straight to the worktable. "Oh boy, pies! When can we have one?"

"Tomorrow at the picnic, Grandpa. Hands off." Bernice batted at his hand.

Grandpa cackled with delight and winked at Billie. "Maybe I'll sneak one out to the barn. Care to join me?"

"Maybe you'll pull back a stump where your hand once was." Bernice wagged a finger at him.

Billie laughed. "I'd be careful if I were you, sir. She does have access to knives."

Grandpa and Bernice laughed. "Hey, little Missy," Grandpa said. "Is your betrothed joinin' us for supper?"

"Yes, he is." Billie's cheeks grew hot.

"Great. I want to see if there's any news about that harpy Ferguson's niece."

"Grandpa!" Bernice said in shock. "Don't be name-calling."

"Mrs. Ferguson has a niece?" Billie said, ignoring Bernice's scold.

"Yep. I heard down at the livery her niece is comin' for a visit. Supposed to be a right pretty gal. Be good for that gossipy busybody to have some kin around. Ever since her husband died, she's had nothin' better to do but poke her nose into everyone else's business."

"Grandpa, stop it." Bernice waved a fork at him.

Grandpa chuckled. It was obvious he liked riling Bernice up. "If she gets into town right quick, she can come to the picnic. And that means another lady friend for you, oh granddaughter of mine."

Bernice smiled and rolled her eyes. "That's all well and good, Grandpa. But you can't keep referring to the girl's aunt as a gossiping busybody harpy."

"Regardless of the truth of it," Billie added before she could stop herself.

"Billie!" Bernice objected. "See, Grandpa? You're a bad influence on her."

He shrugged and poked one of the pies. "Ouch! Still too hot."

"Serves you right—I said they were for tomorrow," Bernice said. "Now get out of my kitchen. Find Warren and see if he needs help with anything." She shooed him toward the back door.

"Oh, all right." Grandpa headed for it. "I think he's in the barn."

"He was last I saw him," Bernice said. "Now get."

Billie giggled as the old man left the house, cackling all the way. "He's quite the character."

"Is he ever," Bernice agreed. She cocked her head. "Have you heard anything about Mrs. Ferguson having a niece come to visit?"

"Until now I didn't know she had a niece. I wonder how old she is."

"I should have asked Grandpa. I will at supper." Bernice glanced around the kitchen. "I think we're done for now."

Billie smiled. "I'll put on the kettle for tea."

Lucien stared at Billie across the table, as he'd been doing throughout supper. She wondered if she would ever stop blushing.

Tomorrow was the picnic. She was excited about that, but not as excited as she was about the drive home tonight. A week ago she'd fought with herself over whether Lucien had any real feelings toward her. How could he, given what she was? But as the truth emerged, so did her heart. In a couple of days they would be husband and wife. She could really let her heart soar then.

"Lucien, would you like more pot roast?" Bernice asked.

"Don't mind if I do." He reached for the serving fork. "So things are ready for tomorrow?"

"As ready as they're going to be," Warren said. "I'm sure you passed a few folks on your drive out."

"Yes, as a matter of fact, I did."

"Folks were bringing chairs, tables, that sort of thing. Grandpa and I will get them set up tomorrow morning."

"Would you like some help?" He looked at Billie. "I don't mind coming out early if you don't."

"I don't," she said. "Whatever is needed."

"We could use the extra hands," Warren said. "Thank you, Lucien, Billie." He took another bite of his supper.

Billie did the same. Bernice's pot roast was very good, better than she could make. "Don't forget to write down the recipe for me," she reminded her.

"I will, right after dessert."

Lucien's head came up. "Dessert?"

Billie smiled at the excitement in his eyes. The man did love his food. "We made sugar cookies."

"No pie?" Grandpa whined.

Bernice rolled her eyes "Grandpa…"

"I didn't touch them!" He held his hands up for emphasis. "I'm innocent!"

"He threaten to stuff himself with pies in the barn again?" Warren asked, and eyed his grandfather.

"Yes," Bernice said. "And asked Billie along to help."

Billie giggled. After she and Lucien were married, she planned on spending more time with her new friends. The other women in town were nice to have tea with and chat about this and that, but Bernice was teaching her practical domestic skills—cooking, sewing, mending. Especially cooking—it wouldn't do to have her husband famished.

"How does the dress look?" Lucien asked.

There went the blushing again. Was this going to happen every time he spoke? She felt like a silly schoolgirl. "You'll have to wait and see."

He smiled over his mashed potatoes. "What if I can't wait?"

"You do realize," Warren cut in, "that we'll have to stop the picnic cleanup and come to town for your wedding?" He sliced into his pot roast. "The things I do for friends." Everyone laughed.

"I'll come too," Grandpa said. "This young pup's bound to forget the cleanup and go straight to the weddin'."

"Stop it, you two," Bernice said. "Everyone will pitch in after the picnic. There won't be anything to do the day after except attend the wedding." She nodded curtly to end the conversation.

Billie laughed.

"What's so funny?" Bernice asked.

"You. You could captain a ship."

"Captain Bernice?" Warren said. "Heaven help us all."

"A pirate captain, maybe," Grandpa muttered, then straightened in his chair. "Oh wait—that'd be your ma. Since the woman don't share pies with anyone, she'd never share her buried treasure."

Laughter filled the table as Billie took another bite of pot roast. Her life had changed dramatically over the last week, and all because she now saw the truth. Beauty really was in the eye of the beholder. Each time she looked into Lucien's eyes, she saw the truth more and more, and she liked what she saw.

A good thing, too. She still wasn't fond of what stared back at her in a mirror. But so long as Lucien was, she could be happy. In time, maybe she'd like what she saw, especially her face. Her poor face…would her scars fade over time, or just start hiding behind wrinkles? She didn't know. She only knew that to make their marriage work, she would have to learn to look in the mirror and like what looked back. How could Lucien love someone who didn't love herself?

That was the conclusion she'd come to, but it was easier said than done. She still had conflicting emotions, still woke up in the middle of the night sometimes wondering who she was. Lucien's attentions were so foreign, so out of place. But they were real.

Two more days, Billie, and you'll be married. Let your love grow naturally. Stop being afraid—you're already in love...

"Oh, my goodness," she whispered.

"What?" Bernice asked.

Billie met Lucien's gaze. *Good heavens! I am in love!*

"Billie?" he said with concern. "Something wrong, sweetheart?"

Billie swallowed hard and smiled. "No, not at all."

The day of the picnic dawned clear and bright. The morning air was crisp and Billie wondered if she shouldn't run back upstairs and fetch her shawl.

"You're up early," Mrs. Ferguson said as she took up her post behind the hotel's front counter.

"I'm waiting for Lucien. We're going to help the Johnsons set up for the picnic."

"Yes, the picnic. I'd help, but I have to wait for my niece. She's coming in on the morning stage."

Billie smiled. "Is she staying long?"

"Depends on whose head she turns," Mrs. Ferguson said with a smile of her own. She pulled out a pen and ink and opened the register. "She'll be helping me here in the hotel. Even after she marries, she can still help.

I plan to teach her everything I know, so she and her husband can take the place over."

"A sound plan. I'm sure your niece will be very happy here."

Mrs. Ferguson arched an eyebrow. "Do you?"

Billie's brow furrowed. "Of course."

Mrs. Ferguson smiled again and went back to writing.

Billie watched her a moment, suddenly worried. Did the woman still plan to spread gossip about her? But almost everyone in town knew her story by now. What would it matter?

Lucien walked into the hotel, eyes bright. "There's my future bride. Ready?"

Billie smiled. Mrs. Ferguson, she noticed, didn't. "Is it very cold?"

"Hmmm, yes. Give me your key and I'll fetch your shawl for you."

"Thank you, but I…"

"I don't mind." He held out his hand.

Billie smiled, pulled her key from her reticule and handed it to him. He bounded up the stairs as she giggled in response.

"My my, someone's in a hurry," Mrs. Ferguson commented.

"Yes," Billie said, still watching the staircase.

"In a hurry to get through the day, no doubt."

Billie looked at her. "Perhaps," she said. After all, tomorrow was their wedding day. She wouldn't mind if the day hurried along.

"People sometimes do when they're faced with something they dread."

Billie's stomach tightened. "I beg your pardon?"

Mrs. Ferguson shrugged. "When I'm faced with something unpleasant, I want to get it over and done with, don't you?"

Billie faced her. "What are you talking about?"

Mrs. Ferguson glanced at the staircase. "Come now, my dear. Really."

Billie opened her mouth to comment when Lucien hurried down the stairs, shawl in hand. "Here you are." He wrapped it around her shoulders. "Shall we be off?"

Billie continued to glare at the proprietress, who busied herself with the register once more. "Yes, let's."

They left, went to the buggy and Lucien helped her up. Billie fought the seeds of doubt that Mrs. Ferguson had tried to drop into her heart. She'd obviously been talking about their wedding, and how dare she? Who would say such a thing?

"You all right?" Lucien asked as he sat beside her.

"Yes," she said, dredging up a smile. "Mrs. Ferguson was just being…herself. Let's go."

He smiled, slapped the lines and they were off.

Billie glanced over her shoulder at the hotel, still pondering Mrs. Ferguson's words. Grandpa was right—the woman really was a gossiping old harpy. But Nellie Davis had been too, and to some extent Charlotte. The latter had clearly reformed, and the former was working on it. Maybe a long visit from her niece was just what the woman needed.

Chapter Nineteen

"And this is Summer Riley and her sister-in-law Elle," Bernice said.

Billie smiled at the two women. "I've heard so much about you. It's nice to meet you at last."

The two blondes exchanged a quick look. "Oh dear," Summer said. "I do hope you didn't hear too many things."

"Would it matter?" Billie asked. "I assure you, everything I was told was good."

"That's a relief," Elle said with a laugh. "Our mother-in-law must have done all the talking."

"I heard a few things from Charlotte Quinn as well," Billie admitted. "Also good. I'm sure you'll sleep easy tonight."

The women laughed at her joke. "Has anyone seen Mrs. Ferguson?" Summer asked.

"Why?" Billie asked as a twinge of dread went up her spine.

"I heard her niece was arriving in town today," Elle said. "Nowhere is so small, we get excited whenever anyone visits or comes to stay. We were very excited to meet you."

"Everyone has been so kind to me," Billie said. "I look forward to visiting with you in the future."

"You and Lucien *must* come to our farm for supper once you're married," Summer suggested.

"We'd like that very much," Billie said with a smile.

"Jumpin' Jehoshaphat!" Grandpa cried from several yards away. "Will you look at that?"

The women turned to see Mrs. Ferguson being helped down from the Quinns' wagon by Mr. Quinn. Then he helped a girl—make that *young woman*. Men and a few women began to gather around them, Bernice among them.

"Your wait appears to be over," Billie told Summer. "That must be the niece."

"Come on, Billie," Grandpa said, offering her his arm. "Let's go say howdy. You gals want to join us?"

"Of course," Summer said, following Grandpa and Billie into the growing crowd. "My goodness, you'd think none of us had ever seen a stranger before."

"Billie, can you see her?" Grandpa asked.

"Hard to miss." Billie, a good head taller than most of the townsfolk, could see very well. Mrs. Ferguson's niece was also tall—though not as tall as she was—with a willowy build. Her blonde hair was piled on her head, her face framed by tiny ringlets. Her eyes were large and green and beautiful with dark lashes. She was a stunning beauty, like a blonde Isabella Weaver.

"Well?" Grandpa said. "What do you see?"

"A pretty girl," she said calmly. She also saw Lucien, on the other side of the crowd, staring…no, *gawking* at the newcomer, along with the other men. She'd seen those same looks the day she arrived in town, aimed at Isabella Weaver. The difference was, Mrs. Ferguson's niece was unmarried.

Billie looked hard at Lucien, who stood stunned next to Warren. Bernice, not far away, looked as annoyed as Billie felt.

"Everyone," Mrs. Ferguson said loudly to those not able to get close enough. "May I introduce you to my niece, Miss Ottilie Ferguson." Everyone began to talk at once, welcoming the beauty to Nowhere.

Billie, feeling suddenly self-conscious, stepped back, treading on Grandpa's feet. They stumbled over each other and went down in a heap.

"Billie, Mr. Johnson!" Elle cried as she raced over to help.

"Mr. Johnson, are you all right?" Summer asked as she pulled the old man up.

"No harm done, I'm fine. How about you, Billie?"

Billie sat on the hard ground, her face red with embarrassment. "No injury save my pride."

Bernice made her way through the crowd and took her hand. Elle took the other and together, they pulled her to her feet. "Are you sure you're all right?" Bernice asked.

"Quite fine. I'm glad you managed to make it to Warren. Being small and thin, you have the advantage over me in slipping through crowds."

"And you have the advantage in being able to see over them," Bernice pointed out.

"Handy as all that is," Grandpa said, "I still ain't met the newcomer."

"I can remedy that," Mrs. Ferguson said as she cut

through the crowd, her niece in tow. "Ottilie, let me introduce you to the Johnsons and Rileys."

Ottilie smiled shyly at Grandpa. "Pleased to meet you, sir."

He took her hand and gave it a healthy shake. "Nice to meet you. Plannin' to stay long?"

The girl opened her mouth to speak, but was cut off by her aunt. "That all depends on what sort of offers we get."

"Offers?"

"Of marriage, of course," Mrs. Ferguson stated.

"But Auntie, I didn't come here to get…"

"Of course you did, dear."

Ottilie looked confused, then smiled weakly at the crowd.

"I'm Summer Riley, and this is my sister-in-law Elle."

The girl smiled again, then caught sight of Billie. Her eyes rounded to platters and she gasped.

Billie smiled. She was used to that reaction. "Hello, I'm Billie Sneed. Soon to be Mrs. Billie Miller." She offered the girl a hand, as so many others had.

She took it warily, her eyes on Billie's face, and shook it. "Pleased to meet you, Miss Sneed. I've…heard a lot about you."

Billie raised an eyebrow. "You have?" She looked at Mrs. Ferguson, who met her stare.

"Y-yes," she stammered, pulled her hand out of Billie's and put it behind her back. Billie almost expected her to wipe it on her skirts. She looked at Mrs. Ferguson again, who now wore a smug look on her face.

"How do you find Nowhere?" Bernice asked.

"I'm afraid I haven't seen much of it," she said. "As

soon as my things were in my room, Mr. and Mrs. Quinn fetched us here."

"I'm sure you'll find it quite charming," Billie said.

The girl's eyes suddenly lit up. "Are you from England?"

"Yes, I am."

"London?" the girl asked.

Mrs. Ferguson cleared her throat. "There will be time for questions later, Ottilie. I want to introduce you to some more people. Oh, Mr. Davis!" She grabbed her niece by the hand and dragged her away.

"That wasn't very polite," Bernice stated.

"No, it wasn't," Billie agreed. She looked for Lucien again but didn't see him. Probably a good thing—she didn't need to feel doubtful. She had a strange feeling in her belly and she didn't like it.

"Let's go fetch the rest of the lemonade and put it on the table," Bernice said.

Billie nodded and followed her toward the house. "Mrs. Ferguson's niece is…pretty."

Bernice glanced at her over one shoulder as she climbed the porch steps. "Yes, she is. But I don't know what put it in Mrs. Ferguson's head to marry her off while she's here. There are no eligible bachelors in town right now except a few early-arriving fruit-pickers."

Billie stopped in the middle of the porch steps and looked at the townspeople milling around. "That is curious. Why would she say such a thing?"

"That girl is young—sixteen at most. The only one around here even close to her age would be Isabella's brother Alfonso, and he's maybe fifteen. Certainly not ready for marriage. I hope they're able to come—though frankly, I won't mind if they don't."

Billie giggled. She'd heard stories over the last couple of weeks about the Weaver clan and the trouble they'd caused in the past. "Do they know about the picnic?"

"Oh, I'm sure they do. Mrs. Gunderson who runs the stage stop would have told them at some point. They pick their mail up there."

"I wouldn't mind seeing Isabella again and meeting her family," Billie said. Maybe a wagonload of Weavers would take her mind off her growing feeling that all was not right with the world.

"If they come, they might not show up until later. Then they'll spend the night with Matthew and Charlotte. It can be a lot of trouble for all of them to get here. But they all show up at the Harvest Festival—Mary Weaver sells her hats there."

"When is the festival?" Billie asked as they entered the house.

"October. It's a lot of fun, you'll see." They went into the kitchen and each carried out a pitcher of lemonade. "We'll have to make more, but not for a while yet," Bernice said. "Are you ready to eat?"

"Yes, but I'll eat when Lucien does." She glanced around as two more wagons came down the lane. "I don't see him anywhere."

"He'll turn up. Lucien's probably with Warren—he likes showing off his livestock."

Billie smiled as she continued searching. "You don't mind if I go find him, do you?"

"Of course not, go ahead. I'll check the food tables. I think we're ready to eat."

Billie nodded goodbye, then began to make her way through the crowds. She'd worn her purple traveling outfit—it was sturdy and pretty. If she'd be sitting on the ground, she didn't want to ruin a good day dress.

To her dismay, she found Lucien sitting under a tree on a blanket with Mrs. Ferguson and her niece. That feeling of dread hit again, sending a shiver up her spine. Lucien looked thoroughly engaged as he spoke with the young woman. Mrs. Ferguson looked just as smug as before, watching them with calculated interest.

Billie could calculate too, and the sum she came up with made her wish she could keel-haul the hotelier. *So that's what you have in mind, you craven Xanthippe—we'll see about that!* She squared her shoulders and marched to where they sat. "Hello, Lucien," she said, then, "Hello again," to Ottilie. She said nothing to Mrs. Ferguson, instead sitting on the blanket next to Lucien and taking his hand.

Mrs. Ferguson frowned and turned to Lucien. "How long have you worked at the bank again?"

"About four years now," he said, patting Billie's hand. "But you already know that, Mrs. Ferguson."

"Oh yes, so I do." She giggled. "Ottilie is very good with numbers, which will come in handy when she takes over the hotel for me."

Ottilie jerked in surprise, her eyes widening. "But Auntie…"

"Don't speak until you're spoken to, dear," Mrs. Ferguson snapped.

Ottilie closed her mouth and gave Billie a helpless look.

Billie shrugged. The poor girl. Mrs. Ferguson was very obviously using her to entice Lucien. She almost laughed, but knew that Mrs. Ferguson thought she could, because she assumed Lucien couldn't be attracted to Billie. A week ago she might have thought the same—but now she just swatted the doubts aside and plotted her next move.

"Ottilie is also very good at needlework and sewing," Mrs. Ferguson prattled on. "She's going to make some lucky man a wonderful wife soon."

"Soon," Lucien repeated, leaning slightly toward Billie.

"Of course." Mrs. Ferguson looked at Billie. "Probably sooner than we think."

"Auntie…"

"Ottie, mind your manners," Mrs. Ferguson scolded. She smiled at Lucien. "Ottie is her nickname."

Lucien smiled and gave her niece a polite nod.

Billie sighed. This girl didn't have a prayer if Mrs. Ferguson was pushing her to marry soon…of course! It had taken her a second to realize it, but the old biddy had given her a perfect opening. "Why, that's wonderful!" she enthused, looking at Ottilie. "It will be so nice to have another newlywed around."

Ottilie hesitated, but she had been spoken to. "Another newlywed?"

"Oh yes, did your aunt tell you? Lucien and I are marrying tomorrow!"

Next to her, she could feel every muscle in Lucien's body relax. "We are so looking forward to it. It would be lovely if you could attend."

"Oh, I'd love to!" Ottilie replied. "Could we, Auntie?"

Before Mrs. Ferguson could respond, there was a sudden commotion as more wagons came down the lane. "Great jumpin' horny toads!" someone cried. "The Weavers are here!"

Lucien straightened. "Oh dear."

Mrs. Ferguson blanched. "Quick, protect Ottie! I won't have any of those heathens corrupt my niece!"

"As opposed to you doing it?"

Billie's heart leaped at the sound of Nellie Davis's voice. For some reason, she felt as if the Light Brigade had just arrived. "Nellie, you came."

"Of course I came, dear. I wouldn't miss this for the world. Unfortunately I've already lost my husband—have any of you seen him?"

"Never mind about Mr. Davis," Mrs. Ferguson cried. "Someone hide Ottie!"

"Mrs. Ferguson, calm yourself," Lucien said.

"Quick, Lucien, take her to the house! Hide her in a bedroom upstairs!" She struggled to her feet, pulling her niece up with her, and shoved her at Lucien.

But her aim was off, and Ottilie went sprawling—right into Billie's lap.

"Lucien Miller!" Mrs. Ferguson screeched. "What are you doing?"

At that moment, Lucien was sitting there in confusion, still holding Billie's hand, his eyes flicking between his sweetheart and his tormentor. "Ma'am?"

Billie, knowing what was up, moved Ottilie to sit on her other side. "Don't worry about the Weavers—from what I've heard they can get a bit rowdy, but they mean no harm."

Mrs. Ferguson, meanwhile, hadn't grasped that her ploy had failed. "Take your hands off of my niece this instant, Lucien!"

"My hands aren't on her, Mrs. Ferguson."

Nellie Davis just scoffed. "Connie, that's got to be one of the oldest tricks in the book. The least you can do is be competent at it."

Billie stifled a giggle. Ottilie just looked confused.

"How can you joke at a time like this?" Mrs. Ferguson shouted, drawing a crowd. Which was obviously her intent. "Lucien, what do you have to say for yourself?"

Lucien climbed to his feet. "I beg your pardon, but why did you shove your niece into my fiancée?"

Billie beamed at his use of *fiancée*.

"I did nothing of the kind. You snaked your arms around her and pulled her on top of you. I saw it."

"Oh for Heaven's sake," Billie muttered. "We all saw you pushed her."

"Why did you do that, Auntie?" Ottilie asked.

"And why do you think you'll get away with that cock-and-bull story when you've got four witnesses who know you're making it up?" Nellie added. "Now stop this nonsense before you scare your niece half to death. I declare, she'll want to be on the first stage out of town."

Mrs. Ferguson began to turn an interesting shade of red.

Billie stood, helped Ottilie up, and took her hand and Lucien's. "Let's go get some lemonade, shall we?" Both nodded and allowed Billie to lead them through the crowd to the refreshment tables.

"My aunt is acting strangely," Ottilie said. "I apologize for her behavior."

"It's all right," Billie replied. "I know what she's up to. She wants you to be married, but at the moment Nowhere is a bit short of eligible bachelors. So she was hoping to swipe mine for you."

Lucien pulled up short. "She was?!" He looked back in alarm, then turned to Billie. "Oh dear, I'm sorry, darling—I didn't realize until now… I would never…"

Now Ottilie was confused. "But Auntie said I should marry you, that you'd make a fine husband."

Billie bit her tongue momentarily to stop a rather sharp response. "Well, I think he shall as well. But he and I are getting married tomorrow—correct?"

"Absolutely," Lucien replied. "Your aunt told you that I was available?"

"Yes. She wrote to me about you, and said you were the most eligible bachelor in town. She was quite adamant that I come to Nowhere so I could meet you. I'm way too young to marry, I think, but she was so insistent."

Billie's jaw trembled. She was so angry she wanted to cry. But she knew the harpy's words were lies—looking in Lucien's eyes, feeling his hand in hers, was all the proof she needed.

Chapter Twenty

"**M**iss Sneed!"

Billie, Lucien and Ottilie turned to see Isabella Weaver making her way toward them, a line of dark-haired children following behind like ducklings. "Mrs. Weaver." She forced a smile. Mrs. Ferguson's machinations had now been scotched, she was sure, but it had taken a lot out of her.

"Miss Sneed," Isabella repeated when she reached her. "I am so happy to see you again. Look." She turned to the group of beauties behind her. "My brothers and sisters all want to meet you!"

Billie fought a sigh, but Lucien chuckled. *Yes, easy for you to laugh—you don't stand out in a crowd like I do.*

The eldest sibling approached—Rufina, wasn't it?—with a little girl clinging to her skirt. "Miss Sneed, I've looked forward to seeing you again," she said with awe in her eyes.

"It's nice to see you again too."

Rufi smiled and looked at the little one attached to

her. "This is Gabriella. We call her Gabby. She especially wanted to meet you."

Billie bent down to look at the child. "Hello."

Gabby smiled widely. "You're wonderful!"

Billie wasn't sure what to make of that. "Er...really?"

Gabby nodded. She glanced around, then motioned Billie closer. "Is he dead?"

"What?"

"The man who gave you those scars. Or was it a big beast?"

Billie heard Lucien working hard to stay silent. It was funny, though. "No, he's not dead that I know of."

"You're very brave. I want to be brave too, just like you."

Billie swallowed hard and straightened up.

"Gabby, what did you say?" Rufi asked.

"Nothiiiing," Gabby said, swaying to and fro.

"I'm sorry if she was impolite," Isabella said. "Mrs. Gunderson at the stage stop was telling us about..." She stopped and smiled at Billie. "... 'the brave woman with the scars' who came to Nowhere. The children could not get here fast enough."

Billie watched the child, who still had that look of wonder in her eyes. "The woman with the scars..."

Two boys approached, both gaping as well. "Do you have a sword?" one asked.

"Leo!" Rufi said. "Don't ask silly questions. This is a lady from England, not a, a..."

"Not a pirate?" the other boy said. He sounded disappointed.

"Arturo!" Isabella warned. "Mind your manners!"

Now Billie had to keep from laughing. "No, I don't

have a sword. But my father was a ship's captain. And
I have met a few pirates—"

"Can we see it?" another girl, twelve or thirteen,
asked.

Billie knew what they wanted. "It would be too much
for you."

"No, it wouldn't," the girl insisted.

"Stop it, all of you!" Rufina growled, then turned
to Billie. "I am so sorry. They are like untrained animals at times."

"They're children and curious," Billie said. She
glanced around, then bent down so the younger ones
could hear. "I was attacked by a horrible man while protecting my father. That's how I got these scars."

"Do you have an eye under there?" Gabby asked,
pointing at Billie's eyepatch.

"No, I lost it."

The girls gasped. The boys were mesmerized.

Rufi shrugged. "If you show them, you'll be their
hero and they'll follow you the rest of the day. You'll
never be rid of them."

Hero? Billie smiled. "Well, there are worse things."
She flipped up her eyepatch.

The children oohed and ahhed. Two of the boys even
clapped. Ottilie gulped. Well, you couldn't please everyone.

"That's enough," Isabella said. "You are to act like
young ladies and gentlemen."

"But she showed us!" the youngest boy whined.

Billie replaced her eyepatch. "Because you asked.
Now you've seen it."

"Are you getting married?" Gabby blurted.

Billie's heart went to her toes and back. Her reaction came out of nowhere, like a ghost come to haunt her. Maybe Mrs. Ferguson had done more damage than she'd thought…

"Yes," Lucien said, taking her hand and beaming. "Tomorrow she's marrying me."

Rufi and the twelve-year-old sighed.

"We would like to attend the wedding if it is all right with you," Isabella said. "I told you we would when I saw you last."

"Yes, you did." Billie saw the children around her. "All of you are invited—I look forward to having you there."

Gabby began to jump up and down. "Yay!" She grabbed Billie by the hand. "Can I eat with you?"

"Us too!" one of the other girls cried.

"Let go of Miss Sneed!" Isabella ordered over their excited giggles.

"They're all right," Billie said. That the children were so excited to eat with her came as a shock. Most children took one look at her and ran, and lately she'd automatically avoided crossing paths with little ones because of it. But not these children.

And more were coming. "Good heavens," she whispered as another batch approached. But these were toddlers, and Calvin Weaver brought up the rear.

Lucien nodded. "There are a *lot* of Weavers."

"Calvin," Isabella smiled. "Look who I found."

"Howdy, Miss Sneed, Luce," Calvin called. "Ya hitched yet?"

"Tomorrow," Lucien replied before Billie could. Silently, Billie thanked him for it. Despite her bravado, Mrs. Ferguson had momentarily derailed the progress she'd made. And it was progress. People didn't change overnight, and she could thank Lucien and her new friends for getting her this far, but it was hard, very hard. She would have to work to keep her mind from thinking the sort of things it was used to, things that said she was nobody, a monster, a discard…

Finally, brethren, whatsoever things are true, whatsoever things are honest, whatsoever things are just, whatsoever things are pure, whatsoever things are lovely, whatsoever things are of good report; if there be any virtue and if there be any praise, think on these things… A chill went up her spine as she recalled the scripture. "Yes, yes…"

"Billie?" She turned. Bernice stood there, a glass in hand. "Lemonade?"

Billie took the glass and had a quick sip. "Thank you. Oh, and could we get a glass for Ottilie? This is Mrs. Ferguson's niece of legend."

Ottilie blushed to her roots.

"I want lemonade!" Gabby yelled.

Bernice smiled nervously—a logical reaction to a tidal wave of Weavers. "Follow me—the lemonade is over here."

Calvin snatched up two of the toddlers—identical twins, possibly. "Come on, sugar, I'll get you some lemonade."

Gabby looked up at Billie with wide eyes. "You're coming too, aren't you?"

"Of course," Lucien said, then leaned over to Billie. "That way, both of us will be too busy to give Constance Ferguson the horse-whipping she so richly deserves, eh, sweetheart?"

Billie laughed out loud—she couldn't help it.

As they walked, Lucien surveyed the myriad Weavers. "Alfonso, you've grown! Are you old enough to work at the bank yet?"

The oldest boy smiled. "Not yet, sir. Soon."

"When?"

"I'm fifteen."

Lucien nodded. "Give it another year, then."

Alfonso smiled widely and glanced at Calvin. "Did you hear that?"

"I heard. Don't let your sister hear, though."

Billie blinked a few times. "Why not?"

"Al here's good with figgers," Calvin said quietly as Isabella chased one of the other girls. "Lucien told him they could use him at the bank when he's old enough, but Isabella's kinda…protective. She don't wanna let him go just yet."

"The boy is sharp, though," Lucien said. "Hungry?"

Billie nodded and fought the urge to hold on to him.

He sensed her distress. "I'll fix us each a plate while you tend to your admirers—and Ottilie. I think she could use a friend, not to mention a bulwark against her aunt." His eyes narrowed. "Are you all right?"

She smiled at him. "With you here, yes, I am."

"I am here, Billie. And after we're married tomorrow, I always will be." He kissed her on the cheek.

Billie's chest heaved. All her doubts and fears, hopes and dreams crashed together like giant waves, her heart in the middle. Unbelief, she concluded, was a powerful force. The question was, did she believe him? To do so, she'd have to fight. But it was a fight she wanted, and she was willing. She looked him in the eyes and smiled defiantly. "Yes, I know. Go get our food."

* * *

Tarnation! What was that fool Mrs. Ferguson think-ing? Lucien thought as he headed for the food tables. How dare that old busybody torture Billie—and her poor niece—like that?

Speaking of which, there she was talking with Mary Weaver—correction, Mary *Hughes*—and her husband Harlan. "And that's the truth of it!" she brayed as he approached. Mary and Harlan gave him an odd look, then glanced at Mrs. Ferguson. Wonderful.

"Hello, Harlan, Mary. How are things out at the farm?"

"Just as fine as they can be, Lucien," Harlan said. "No one's been tossed down a well in months. I count that as progress."

Lucien laughed.

"So," Mary asked, "where's your bride to be? I'd like to meet her."

Mrs. Ferguson pressed her lips together. "Mary!"

"Don't 'Mary' me, Connie. I don't buy a word of it."

Lucien's eyes narrowed at Mrs. Ferguson. "What have you been telling these people?"

The woman's mouth opened and closed like a freshly caught trout's.

"She says her niece came to town and 'suffered an altercation'," Harlan volunteered.

Lucien smiled. The woman should know better than to tangle with Weavers, even a Weaver by marriage. And especially Harlan Hughes, a retired sheriff. "Go on."

"Yep—says your bride threatened her."

"What?!" Lucien turned on Mrs. Ferguson. "Now see

here, madam, I've had enough of your lies for one day. I don't know what's in your craw, but I'll not have it."

Mrs. Ferguson squared her shoulders. "I'll tell you, Lucien Miller, you're an idiot to marry a woman the likes of that…that Sneed girl. Why, no one will visit you, you'll never entertain, you'll be the laughing stock of the entire territory!"

Lucien stood in shock, as did the other onlookers. One of which was Billie, who'd apparently decided to find out what was taking him so long. She marched up like the avenging goddess he'd imagined she could be, until she leaned over Connie Ferguson like a cliff about to fall on her. "If you have anything further to say about me, Mrs. Ferguson, then kindly say it to my face. If you dare."

"Face," Mrs. Ferguson scoffed. "*That* face…"

"Is beautiful," Lucien said. "Why on Earth does it bother you so much?"

Mrs. Ferguson's face became pinched. "My niece will take over the hotel for me one day. I want her married to someone decent! I had it all planned until *you* came along!" She glared at Billie.

Billie looked at Lucien in…was it *amusement*? "Were you aware of this?"

"Of course not—I would have stopped it in a moment if I was." Lucien shook his head at Mrs. Ferguson. "Great Scott, woman, have you gone completely mad? You can't plan someone else's life for them."

"My niece doesn't know what's best for her!" Mrs. Ferguson clenched her fists. "Look at her!" she said with a nod at Billie. "This…thing you're going to marry. Why, when you could have Ottilie?"

Compassion filled Billie as she realized what was

really happening. "You don't hate me. You're afraid of something."

Mrs. Ferguson covered her mouth. "How dare you! What do you know?"

Billie's voice was soft as a spring breeze. "Trust me, I know about being afraid. What is it?"

To everyone's surprise, Mrs. Ferguson burst into tears. "My hotel! It's all I have left! I don't want it to go to some stranger!"

Lucien and Billie exchanged a look with Mary and Harlan.

"Everything all right?" a deep voice asked as Arlan Weaver pushed his way through the crowd.

"That's what I'd like to know." Lucien wrapped his arm around Billie, thinking to protect her.

But she had other ideas. "Let go. There's something wrong—something I can help with."

Lucien took one look at the sobbing Mrs. Ferguson and did.

Billie went to the woman and took her in her arms. "Mrs. Ferguson, it's all right. I understand. But you don't have to be afraid. Why do you believe these things about your hotel? Can you predict the future? I can't."

Lucien had a sense Billie was speaking to herself as much as she was to Mrs. Ferguson.

"My husband and I had that hotel for years. Then he left me!"

The people around watched in shock. They'd never seen the hotel proprietress act this way before. Which made him think. How often did he or anyone else go into the hotel to visit her? Did the other ladies in town invite her to tea or take a meal with her? To his knowledge, no one had, himself included. Mrs. Ferguson almost never left the hotel, except for the occasional trip to the mercantile.

"My father left me too," Billie said. "The same way your husband left you."

Silence fell over the crowd and Lucien wondered if they weren't coming to the same conclusion he just had. Mrs. Ferguson was a forgotten widow. He felt a prick of shame at the thought.

"Your father?" Mrs. Ferguson said. She wiped at her tears. "What does your father have to do with anything?"

"He died," Billie said with a shrug. "I told you that. Murdered, if you want the truth of it. You've heard my tale."

Mrs. Ferguson pulled a handkerchief from her sleeve and wiped her nose. "Murdered?"

"It's true," Lucien said. "Billie's a brave woman and a survivor, Mrs. Ferguson." He gave Billie a faint smile. "Listen to her."

Billie smiled back. "Stop thinking the worst," she told her. "If you expect bad things, you get bad things."

"Expect them?" Mrs. Ferguson huffed. "What else am I to expect? The only man in town capable of running my hotel after I'm gone is marrying *you!* Where does that leave me?"

Billie hugged Mrs. Ferguson tighter. "Don't believe it. Don't believe it for a minute."

"Believe what?" the older woman rasped. "Let go of me!"

"You're not thinking big enough."

"What?"

"You're like me. I never thought I'd marry. I never imagined someone like Lucien was out there, not for me. It took him a lot of work to convince me, him and others."

Mrs. Ferguson looked Billie up and down. "You have to admit, you're a lot for a man to take on."

Billie faced her. "True. Because I *am* a lot of woman. I've sailed the seas, fought bandits, been cut and scarred, lost an eye, traveled across an ocean and a continent. What woman around here can say she's done all that?"

Mrs. Ferguson had the decency to blush. "No one. Though I hear Isabella Weaver is mighty handy at clobbering bandits with a frying pan."

The Weavers present, not to mention a few of the townsfolk, laughed.

Billie put a hand on Mrs. Ferguson's shoulder. "Let us help you figure things out. It's obvious you love your hotel and want good things to happen to it. You don't have to do this alone."

Mrs. Ferguson stared at her. "I've always had to do things alone," she said in a small voice. "Ever since my husband passed years ago."

"Well, if you'd let a body know you needed company," Nellie Davis replied. "There are plenty of us around to help. Land sakes, why didn't you say something?"

"I didn't want to wind up like you," Mrs. Ferguson shot back.

"But you did," Nellie said. "Gossipy and bitter and isolated. But I'm learning to change, and you can too."

"Seems to me there's been enough gossip going on," Harlan commented. "Out on the farm, there's no room for guessing. We have to tell each other how we feel, get things out in the open. You folks need to do the same."

Everyone stared at him. The man was right, Lucien

thought. He looked at Billie. "You know I love you, don't you?"

"Yes. Though you were right about me being thick-headed—it took me far too long to believe it. And I love you, Lucien."

Nellie smiled and looked at Connie Ferguson. "And *you* are joining Charlotte, Abbey and me for tea next week." She turned back to Billie. "That goes for you too, if you're not too busy with your new hubby." She looked at the rest of the townsfolk. "What kind of place is Nowhere if we can't take care of our own? I know I've wronged a lot of you and I've paid the price. But when did we get so busy that none of us noticed what was going on with Connie? I declare, this never should have happened."

Everyone stood in stunned silence at her speech. Except Gabby, who wiggled her way through the crowd and grabbed Billie's wrist. "You're special."

Billie looked at her, a tear in her eye.

"She's right," Lucien said. "I knew it from the moment I set eyes on you." He pulled her away from Mrs. Ferguson and held her close. "I love you, Billie. I've been falling in love with you for days."

Billie choked back a sob. "Lucien," she said as her arms went around him. "I love you too."

Lucien tightened his hold. There were no gasps of shock, no quips about impropriety. It was as if the town had an open wound and Nellie and Billie had just sewn it shut. He looked into Billie's eye and smiled.

"Well, kiss her!" Gabby prompted.

Lucien and Billie looked at the child. "Out of the mouths of babes," Lucien quipped, then looked at his bride and did just that.

* * *

"Oh my goodness, do I look all right?" Billie's voice shook as she spoke.

"I declare, if you don't stand still, I'm going to stick you with a pin!" Nellie said as she worked to fix Billie's veil to her head.

"I'm so nervous. The whole town showed up."

"Of course they did. After yesterday, who wouldn't?" Nellie put the final pin in place. "There, that should hold." She stepped back. "Just look at you—you're a vision. You girls have outdone yourselves."

Charlotte stepped forward. "You're beautiful, Billie."

Billie bit her lip. She was so happy she didn't know what to do with herself. Being worn out from yesterday's picnic didn't help. After the incident with Mrs. Ferguson and the subsequent "meeting of the minds," as Lucien referred to it, everyone wanted to spend time with her. She regaled people with tales of her father, his ship and their life traveling all around Europe.

By the time the picnic was over, she and Lucien had been invited to supper by just about every family in Nowhere, including what Weavers had come. She had yet to meet Daniel and Ebba, Benjamin and Charity and their children. Someone had to stay behind and mind the farm while the rest of the family came to town. She took an immediate liking to Arlan's wife Samijo, who had some interesting tales of her own.

"Are you ready?" Abbey asked as she brushed at Billie's skirt.

"As I'll ever be." She reached up and touched her eyepatch. "I hope I don't get this dirty."

"How can you?"

"I don't know, but I'm sure I'll manage. Are Mrs. Ferguson and Ottilie out there?"

"Yes," Charlotte said. "What you said to her yesterday was a wonderful thing, Billie. If it were me, I'd have had a hard time, but you saw she was hurting. I never noticed until you said something."

"Some of us are better at hiding pain than others," Billie said. "I hid mine so long, I forgot it was there until I saw Lucien for the first time. Then it came at me in a rush."

"I thought I would never change, but I did." Charlotte turned to Nellie. "And Mother, I am so proud of you. I'm sorry I didn't get a chance to tell you yesterday."

Nellie smiled at her daughter. "Don't be too impressed. They say old habits die hard, and I'm sure mine aren't going down without a fight."

"Be that as it may, Mother," Abbey said, "you did the family proud yesterday."

"Thank you, my dears. Now, let's get Billie out there and married."

Abbey slipped out the back room of the church as Charlotte took Billie's hand. "Come, let's get you where you need to be."

Billie followed her out a side door and along the path to the front of the church. She heard an organ begin to play and her heart raced. This was it!

Grandpa Johnson sidled up beside her. "You ready, Missy?"

"Yes. Are you?"

"Always! And may I say, it's an honor to give the bride away."

"Thank you for agreeing to it. I couldn't think of anyone better for the job."

Grandpa smiled as the wedding march began to play. "Congratulations, Billie. And I ain't talkin' about gettin' hitched. I'm talkin' 'bout acceptin' yourself. Took me years."

"It did?" she said quietly as they started down the aisle.

"Yep. My guess is there's lots of folks around here need to do the same. And you're just the gal to help them."

Billie smiled as she met Lucien's gaze. He looked so handsome in his black suit, waiting for her at the altar. "I'll do my best."

"And that's good enough, Billie Jane." They reached Lucien and Pastor Lewis. Grandpa put her hand into Lucien's and smiled. "*And* congratulations on gettin' hitched." With a chuckle, he left them to take a seat.

"What was that about?" Lucien whispered as they turned to face the preacher.

Billie smiled. "You'll see. But let's get married first, hm?"

Lucien gave her hand a squeeze. "Sounds good to me."

Pastor Lewis cleared his throat and their wedding began.

* * * * *

A Note to My Readers...

~🖋

For those of you wondering about Billie the cat, the inspiration for *Dear Mr. Miller*, here is her story. She came to us through Beastie Bestie, a pet store and adoption center in Brooklyn, New York. My daughter wanted to foster a kitty, met Bronwen the owner of Beastie Bestie, and soon Billie entered our lives. A rescue cat, she was in horrible shape when found. She was starving, had had a batch of kittens that were literally sucking the life out of her, and a terrible ear infection. When she came to us the ear infection had been cleared up, she'd put on weight, and was well on the mend. But she wouldn't let you touch her belly, and because of the ear infection, kept her head tilted off to one side. Her balance was off, so she'd not make a mouser, and she didn't do well with other animals. My daughter is a writer/director and fashion photographer. There are production meetings, photo shoots and such going on at her apartment all the time. At first Billie was shy around the models, stylists, designers and musicians that often come to the apartment. But soon, she took to all the attention, and after a few weeks was a completely different kitty! She even managed to worm her way into a few shots of a fashion shoot!

Because of her "quirks" there was worry Billie wouldn't get adopted. After all, who wants a cat that won't get along with other pets, has a head tilt, jumps on things and falls off, and won't let a person touch her except on the head? But with lots of love and acceptance, Billie began to change as she began to trust. Now you can hold her, play with her, and she's a furry bundle of love. When it came time to create the heroine for *Dear Mr. Miller*, I took one look at Billie sitting in a chair on the other side of the room, and poof! Billie Jane Sneed was born.

Billie has since gone on to live with her new forever Mommy, but will always be in our hearts. Not to mention in the occasional visit as she lives just done the street! So if you've ever wondered where authors get their inspiration to create their stories, here's just one example. Billie the kitty.

*When a city slicker wants the same piece of land
as a small-town girl, will sparks fly between them?*

Read on for a sneak preview of
Opening Her Heart
by Deb Kastner.

What on earth?

Suddenly, a shiny red Mustang came around the curve of the driveway at a speed far too fast for the dirt road, and when the vehicle slammed to a stop, it nearly hit the side of Avery's SUV.

Who drove that way, especially on unpaved mountain roads?

The man unfolded himself from the driver's seat and stood to his full over-six-foot height, let out a whoop of pure pleasure and waved his black cowboy hat in the air before combing his fingers through his thick dark hair and settling the hat on his head.

Avery had never seen him before in her life.

It wasn't so much that they didn't have strangers occasionally visiting Whispering Pines. Avery's own family brought in customers from all over Colorado who wanted the full Christmas tree–cutting experience.

So, yes, there were often strangers in town.

But this man?

He was as out of place as a blue spruce in an orange grove. And he was on land she intended to purchase—before anyone else was supposed to know about it.

Yes, he sported a cowboy hat and boots similar to those that the men around the Pines wore, but his whole getup probably cost more than Avery made in a year, and his new boots gleamed from a fresh polish.

Avery fought to withhold a grin, thinking about how quickly those shiny boots would lose their luster with all the dirt he'd raised with his foolish driving.

Served him right.

Just what was this stranger doing *here*?

"And didn't you say the cabin wasn't listed yet?" Avery said quietly. "What does this guy think he's doing here?"

"I have no idea how—" Lisa whispered back.

"Good afternoon, ladies," said the man as he tipped his hat, accompanied by a sparkle in his deep blue eyes and a grin Avery could only categorize as charismatic. He could easily have starred in a toothpaste commercial.

She had a bad feeling about this.

As the man approached, the puppy at Avery's heels started barking and straining against his lead—something he'd been in training not to do. Was he trying to protect her, to tell her this man was bad news?

Don't miss
Opening Her Heart *by Deb Kastner,*
available January 2021 wherever
Love Inspired books and ebooks are sold.

LoveInspired.com

LIEXP1220

LOVE INSPIRED
INSPIRATIONAL ROMANCE

UPLIFTING STORIES OF FAITH, FORGIVENESS AND HOPE.

Join our social communities to connect with other readers who share your love!

Sign up for the Love Inspired newsletter at **LoveInspired.com** to be the first to find out about upcoming titles, special promotions and exclusive content.

CONNECT WITH US AT:

 Facebook.com/LoveInspiredBooks

 Twitter.com/LoveInspiredBks

Facebook.com/groups/HarlequinConnection

Get 4 FREE REWARDS!

We'll send you 2 FREE Books plus 2 FREE Mystery Gifts.

Love Inspired books feature uplifting stories where faith helps guide you through life's challenges and discover the promise of a new beginning.

FREE Value Over $20

YES! Please send me 2 FREE Love Inspired Romance novels and my 2 FREE mystery gifts (gifts are worth about $10 retail). After receiving them, if I don't wish to receive any more books, I can return the shipping statement marked "cancel." If I don't cancel, I will receive 6 brand-new novels every month and be billed just $5.24 each for the regular-print edition or $5.99 each for the larger-print edition in the U.S., or $5.74 each for the regular-print edition or $6.24 each for the larger-print edition in Canada. That's a savings of at least 13% off the cover price. It's quite a bargain! Shipping and handling is just 50¢ per book in the U.S. and $1.25 per book in Canada.* I understand that accepting the 2 free books and gifts places me under no obligation to buy anything. I can always return a shipment and cancel at any time. The free books and gifts are mine to keep no matter what I decide.

Choose one: ☐ **Love Inspired Romance Regular-Print** (105/305 IDN GNWC) ☐ **Love Inspired Romance Larger-Print** (122/322 IDN GNWC)

Name (please print)

Address   Apt. #

City   State/Province   Zip/Postal Code

Email: Please check this box ☐ if you would like to receive newsletters and promotional emails from Harlequin Enterprises ULC and its affiliates. You can unsubscribe anytime.

Mail to the **Reader Service:**
IN U.S.A.: P.O. Box 1341, Buffalo, NY 14240-8531
IN CANADA: P.O. Box 603, Fort Erie, Ontario L2A 5X3

Want to try 2 free books from another series? Call 1-800-873-8635 or visit www.ReaderService.com.

---

*Terms and prices subject to change without notice. Prices do not include sales taxes, which will be charged (if applicable) based on your state or country of residence. Canadian residents will be charged applicable taxes. Offer not valid in Quebec. This offer is limited to one order per household. Books received may not be as shown. Not valid for current subscribers to Love Inspired Romance books. All orders subject to approval. Credit or debit balances in a customer's account(s) may be offset by any other outstanding balance owed by or to the customer. Please allow 4 to 6 weeks for delivery. Offer available while quantities last.

Your Privacy—Your information is being collected by Harlequin Enterprises ULC, operating as Reader Service. For a complete summary of the information we collect, how we use this information and to whom it is disclosed, please visit our privacy notice located at corporate.harlequin.com/privacy-notice. From time to time we may also exchange your personal information with reputable third parties. If you wish to opt out of this sharing of your personal information, please visit readerservice.com/consumerschoice or call 1-800-873-8635. **Notice to California Residents**—Under California law, you have specific rights to control and access your data. For more information on these rights and how to exercise them, visit corporate.harlequin.com/california-privacy.

LI20R2